6-11-?

TO: JIM,
HAPPY FATHER'S DAY,

# HORIZONS
# OF
# HEROES

## THE NEXT TWENTY YEARS

ENJOY THE ROAD!!!

Cameron Price

# CAMERON N.A. PRICE

PUBLICATION
CONSULTANTS
We Believe In The Power Of Authors

PO Box 221974 Anchorage, Alaska 99522-1974
books@publicationconsultants.com—www.publicationconsultants.com

ISBN: 978-1-59433-775-8
eISBN: 978-1-59433-776-5
Library of Congress Catalog Card Number: 2018932190

Manufactured in the United States of America.

2

*Horizons of Heroes: The Next Twenty Years* is based on many true stories and events, lightly salted with spice, that happened over forty years ago. The author has tried to recreate events, locales, and conversations from his memories of them. Names of individuals have been changed to protect their privacy. Additionally, he has changed some identifying characteristics and details such as physical properties, occupations, cities, and countries. Although the author and publisher have made every effort to ensure that the information in this book was correct at press time, the author and publisher do not assume and hereby disclaim any liability to any party for any loss, damage, or disruption caused by errors or omissions, whether such errors or omissions result from negligence, accident, or any other cause. Any resemblance to actual person(s), living or dead, is purely coincidental.

# Acknowledgments

T his book was inspired by many good friends and true stories. My readers also deserve sincere praise for requesting Book Two. A special thanks to my editors who helped polish this book.

This book was edited by M. Burkhart, J. Kauranen, M. van der Lende, D. Pool, and J. Price.

# Table of Contents

# Chapter 1

# Welcome Home

S itting in their military aircraft seats, Big El and Cameron laughed hard as they rehashed their many adventures of the past four years. Their friendship had been filled with days of endless laughter, which to them was life's warmest creation. Now, they were about to land back in the "real world," or back on American soil.

The pilot came on the intercom, "Please ensure your seat belts are buckled tightly as we will be on the ground in fifteen minutes. Men, he continued, the Vietnam War is not a popular war, so after we land, change out of your uniform as soon as possible. Good luck to all of you."

The aircraft, carrying 120 airmen, made a sharp dive, then landed smoothly on the tarmac at McGuire Air Force Base in New Jersey. The excited men quickly exited the military aircraft and walked to the large white Administration building, where they would be released from military duty. It was a bright, sunny, and brisk November day in 1972. Cameron and Big El chuckled as they saw one airman drop to his knees and kiss the ground. These men were lucky as they had survived the war which had left more than 58,200 US soldiers killed and over 303,500 wounded. Sadly, nearly 2,600,000 U.S. soldiers were deployed to South Vietnam and the total military and civilian casualties from the United States and Vietnam numbered nearly 5,500,000.

Big El and Cameron were the last airmen to leave the plane. Moments after stepping off the plane, they noticed a large band. It started playing the air force theme song by Robert Crawford:

"Off we go into the wild blue yonder,
climbing high into the sun;
Here they come zooming to meet our thunder,
at 'em boys. Give 'er the gun now!
Down we dive, spouting our flame from under,
Off with one helluva roar!
We live in fame or go down in flame.
Hey! Nothing'll stop the U.S. Air Force!"

Cameron noticed that the band was led by his old friend Doug, from basic training at Lackland Air Force Base in San Antonio, Texas, who had wanted to play the saxophone in the military band. Cameron had helped motivate him to pass the make, or, break timed track event. Failure would have resulted in his washout from the service. Here he was living his dream leading the military band. Cameron smiled at Doug for the very nice honor. Good friends were for life!

"Cam, I have been tracking your locations with the hope that someday I could repay you for saving my career. I am indebted to you forever. I asked the captain, when I learned that you would be coming to McGuire, for permission to lead the band today. Captain obtained approval from the base commander. Cam, you are home, but I have to tell you that you must have done amazing things overseas for the commander to approve the request." With tears flowing down his face, he gave Cameron a big hug. Doug went on to spend 20 years leading military bands throughout the United States. Prior to retiring, he was assigned to the White House. When asked by the President, "What was your greatest moment in your career as the best band instructor in the military?" He replied, "Well, sir, I don't know about being the best, but the answer is easy. If it wasn't for the action of an airman years ago who believed in me and pushed me during basic training, I would not be here."

In the Administration building, Big El and Cameron processed out of the service receiving good conduct awards and honorable discharges. There were no purple hearts, bronze, or silver stars or other medals for them as military spys do not receive such medals. Prior to leaving the building, they walked into a mandatory class on veteran employment opportunities.

"Men, as you transition to civilian life, jobs are going to be difficult to secure. There are three jobs that I urge you to consider: refrigerator repair, air conditioning, and wedding photography. They all pay well and you should have no trouble landing a job in these fields," Big El and Cameron thanked the sergeant for his recommendation.

They walked out of the building, free men. The high fives continued between the men. Then, there she was leaning against Big El's powder blue Camaro muscle car. Susan was absolutely beautiful. Cameron had never seen Big El move so fast as when he ran to Susan. They kissed passionately while he lifted her off the ground twirling her around and around. Her hair and dress twinkling in the sunlight. She started crying as she was so happy. He tried to wipe away her tears but the flood gates had opened.

Cameron was witnessing true love firsthand. Susan and Big El loved each other so much. Months, make that years, of separation had only made their love stronger. Big El slowly put Susan back on the ground and said, "You are the love of my life."

Susan, wiping away the tears, hugged and kissed Cameron on the cheek and said, "Thank you so very much for bringing my Elston back to me."

"Susan," said Cam, "there was absolutely nothing that could have kept Big El from returning to you. I am so happy to share this magic moment watching you both." They all laughed. It was great to be home.

Cameron knew that Big El had given up a possible professional career as a Hollywood comic or movie star to follow his heart. Nothing mattered but Susan.

Susan was a nurse and worked about 10 miles from her parents' house. She had graduated from University of Rhode Island with a nursing degree and was now working at the Rhode Island Hospital. She loved putting smiles on her patients' faces.

"Okay, Cameron, you ride shotgun and Susan, you sit in the middle. We are going to stay at Susan's parents' house for a few days."

Driving his powerful Camaro, it still took approximately four hours to reach Susan's parents' home in rural Rhode Island. Heading up the long asphalt drive-way, Big El suddenly stopped his car and rolled down the window. He yelled, "Sano roo, Nikki, sano roo!" Nikki was a giant Siberian husky who ran up to the car with a wailing greeting: "Sano roo." Everyone jumped out of the car laughing and petting Nikki. Nikki obviously remembered Big El and danced lovingly around him, almost doing flips.

Susan's brother, Larry Junior, came out of the house drinking a beer. Larry worked at a car parts dealership. He knew how to fix cars and make them fly. "What the crap, you made it out of the war alive. Good for you Elston. Nice meeting you Cameron, wanna beer?"

"In a minute," said Cameron.

Next out was Granny. Granny had moved to America from Finland when she was about 19. She was approximately 90 years old now, had a delightful Finnish accent, and moved like a track star. She ran up to Cameron and said enthusiastically, "My favorite drink is peach schnapps. Have you tried schnapps?"

"No," said Cameron.

"I will get you a glass. You will love it."

She ran back into the house.

Next were Betty and Larry Senior. Cameron learned from Larry that they had purchased the nearly twenty-acre lot over 30 years ago and Larry had built the beautiful brick home all by himself. They also built a huge sauna next to a large pond called Schnapps' Pond. The log fire sauna could hold ten people and they could raise the temperature up to approximately 220 degrees. "We will take you down there tonight," said Big El. "To get you mentally prepared, think in terms of having a beer and pouring cold water over a hot fire. The hot steam fills the sauna until you see the Finnish angel called, Lordie Lordie Lordie! Then you walk to the pond, which is now covered in ice. We have to cut a hole in the ice where you jump in. As quickly as you jump in, he continued, "you jump out and run back to the sauna for another beer, and then the process repeats itself."

Betty asked Cameron, "Have you ever had Krispy Cringle? It's a Finnish dish."

"Sounds wonderful," said Cameron with a pleasing smile.

Granny came back with two glasses of peach schnapps. "Here, Cameron, take a slug and let me know what you think." As she sat next to Cameron, she put one arm around him. "My Cameron, you are certainly built strong. Are those muscles all over your body?" She squeezed him with delight.

Cameron laughed, as he could tell that ole' granny liked him. He took a slug of peach schnapps and said, "Granny, this is wonderful!"

Dinner was ready and they were all called to the dinner table. Granny said, "I want Cameron to sit next to me."

Everyone laughed as Granny was a happy lady.

Larry Junior, said, "Hey brother, you my brother from now on."

Cameron asked Larry Senior how he met Betty. He smiled and said, "We first met at a rural formal country ball about 35 years ago. I was wearing a suit, which I hate to wear, and I was loosening my tight collar when I noticed this vision of loveliness. It was Betty. She was wearing a beautiful pink gown and was a very pretty lady. After two or three drinks, I got up the courage to ask her to dance. The band was playing loudly as I approached Betty. I tapped her on her shoulder. I was so nervous that when she turned to look at me that I let out the biggest and loudest fart ever heard, just as the band stopped playing. Everyone, I mean everyone, heard that fart. I smiled, and loudly said, "That is quite all right, my dear. I will tell everyone that it was me that farted." Betty was so embarrassed that she nearly fainted. To say the least, she remembered me when I called on her the next week. She said that she had never laughed so hard and she had to give me a chance. We got married two years later."

Later that night they went down to Schnapps' Pond for a fantastic sauna. The air was crisp and the pond was frozen. They cut a hole in the ice. The Finnish tradition of hot sauna and drinks should be considered by many Americans, as it so relaxing. Larry

Junior brought his girlfriend. "I thought I could drink he said, but Elston and Cameron, you guys can really drink."

Big El said, "After stomping grapes, we became grand connoisseurs of wine and when no wine was available we turned to our favorites, Johnny Walker and Jack Daniels."

The next evening, Susan, Big El, and Cam went to Big El's favorite restaurant, the Oak Plank Brew House, where his friend Happy was working. When Happy saw Big El, he worked his way across the restaurant and said "Elston, I missed you my friend!"

"And I missed you too, Happy," said Big El. "You remember my girlfriend, Susan, and this is my best buddy Cameron. We survived the war together."

"Nice meeting you, Cameron."

"I'm going to take good care of you this evening. Cameron, do you want to taste the best steak and lobster in America?"

"Absolutely and it is great to meet you," Cameron replied.

"Happy, also, please bring us two Jacks and one Johnny Red on the rocks."

"You got it. I will be back in a flash," said Happy, thrilled at seeing an old friend after such a long time.

Cameron walked slowly to the men's room exploring this very special rustic restaurant. The lovely cedar furnishings were beautifully adorned with many plants, trees, and flowers. On the way back he saw Susan and Big El hugging and kissing. Happy had now returned with the drinks so Cam returned to the table. Susan held up a glass and said, "I would like to propose a toast. Here's to the new Mod Squad." The Mod Squad was a 1970s hit TV series featuring a white man and woman and a black man who shared incredible adventures.

"Susan, you may never have realized it, but you made our platoon of 50 service men, some of the happiest men in the world. When our men first saw you by the Administration building in Texas, you gave each of them hope that if they could survive the Vietnam war they might someday find a beautiful woman. Our men did not want to die and you inspired them to serve their country and protect themselves from an early demise."

"Oh, you are so kind," she said, "but I was just a young gal wearing the best outfit I could afford, taking a gamble that I might see Big El, who seemed worth waiting for."

Happy outdid himself as he brought out three 36 ounce steaks and six huge lobsters plus the biggest baked potatoes and salads. Everyone thanked him and ordered more drinks.

When Susan went to the ladies' room, Big El said, "Cam, why don't you live here with us? We could have so much fun together and I am certain you can get a job." Cam knew that Big El really wanted him to stay.

"Big El, I have some unfinished business I must complete. As mentioned in San Sabina, I have to return to Seattle to complete college. Along the way, I want to see Abrianna and maybe Amy to see if the passion is still there. Also, I may look up Sharon to see if I am still in love with her."

"Okay buddy, I understand." Big El leaned over to Cam and whispered, "Do me a favor. If you see Trista, tell her I died in a car accident in Greece. I feel her love and I need it to stop."

"Big El, are you sure? Nothing happened between you two so all you have to do is to tell her it is all over."

"I am sure, buddy, thanks."

"Big El, now it is your turn to show Susan what a great catch and good provider you are going to be by landing that State Trooper's job. Someday, I hope to find love like you have with Susan."

"Elston," said Happy, "the boss says dinner is on us and welcome home!"

Big El, Susan, and Cam all hugged Happy.

Driving up the drive-way at Susan's parent's house, Cameron leaned out the window and yelled, "Sano roo, Nikki, Sano roo! Nikki barked out "sano roo sano roo" and ran up to Cameron.

The next morning after a delicious serving of Krispy Cringle, plus a garlic and onion omelet and a plate of sliced watermelon, Granny gave Cameron a kiss on the cheek. "We will miss you when you leave today and look forward, god willing, to your next visit."

"On your next visit," said Big El, "I want you to meet my side of the family, who live near Boston."

Then Larry Senior, came forward holding an arrow and said, "do you have a moment, Cam?"

Cameron followed him into another room. "As a young man," said Larry. "I got to go hunting for big moose and fishing for king salmon in Alaska. A Native Alaskan gave me this arrow and I want to give it to you. His message and my message to you are simple. In all life's dealings, fly straight as an arrow."

Cameron took the arrow and hugged Larry. "Thank you for your warm hospitality. I promise to fly straight as an arrow. I really look forward to seeing you again."

Cameron's bags were packed and Big El and Susan gave him a ride to the Greyhound station.

The moment had come where they would be going in different directions. This was a day that they had hoped would never come. Now their great friendship would be tested. This could be a very sad moment, but they knew that they would see each other again soon. "Long live Camel," said Cam.

"Amen," said Big El.

On the bus, Cam took out a piece of paper and wrote down the Ten Golden Keys to success that he had learned while serving in the military:

1. Study Karate.
2. Work hard: You can achieve anything you desire, if you are willing to work exceedingly hard and smart for it.
3. Go to college.
4. Dress for success at interviews, looking exactly like the person doing the interviewing.
5. One's aspiration is predicated by using your mental and physical abilities.
6. Never get divorced.
7. Pick your friends by the action of their minds and their hearts.
8. Be a great leader by being smart, honest, having a strong charismatic character, loyal to the team, and developing the team to win.

9. Know true love: It is when time stands still, an irresistible magnetic force moves you to that special someone, and both your heart and mind start dancing in your body, anything short of this is a play date.
10. Be Spiritual.

Cam also wrote down the step to total destruction that he called the Black Skeleton Key No. 1:

# Never do drugs!

He stared out the window thinking about Big El, Susan, and what a wonderful family she had. He thought of the challenges ahead of him and the unknown challenges he would no doubt face. Would it be possible to overcome a .5 college GPA and graduate? A 2.0 GPA is a C average and a .5 is therefore an E plus. Would he find a job? Would he find real love? He pledged to follow the 10 Golden Keys for success and avoid the Black Skeleton key.

The sun was setting and Cameron was in New York City. With its tall buildings and huge population, New York City was the center of "everything" in the world. He could feel the electricity and energy as he got off the bus. Dazzling lights were abundant. Cameron got a room at the Hyatt and called Abrianna. He had not told her that he would be in town. He was very unsure if she would be in town or working in another city with her modeling career.

After several rings, Abrianna answered. "Hi, this is Cam, can you get away?" Oh my, oh my" she said.

"Yes lover, I want to see you now. Where are you?"

"I am at the Hyatt in New York City."

"Ok, get a taxi and meet me at Cara Mia Italian restaurant at 220 Queens Village. Cam, I have to catch a plane at 5:30 a.m. tomorrow morning heading for a photo shoot in Brazil. They are paying me an incredible amount of money, but I will pass if you want me to stay."

"Don't be silly, make the money," Cam said.

As the cab pulled up to the restaurant, he saw Abrianna. Although black women are very sexy and beautiful, Abrianna was arguably the finest woman of any race. Cameron's heart was beating to the steps of a goddess walk. Six feet tall, elegant, impeccably fine features, chocolate satin skin, long hair, lips that pleaded for just one kiss. God just one kiss. Her revealing cleavage in a lovely white lace dress was more than stunning, it was stunningly beautiful. Hugging and kissing passionately, they heated up the street of Queens. They weren't very interested in food but ordered a small salad and no drinks.

"Cameron, would you do me a favor?

"Yes, anything, what is it?"

"I promised an owner of a brand-new nightclub that I would visit his club tonight. He really wants me to be there." Laughing she said, "he told me he wants a beauty enhancer for his high-end clientele. He is paying me $500 to just show up for an hour. But you should know that if we go, my roommate will be home later and we won't be able to go to my place. When I return from Brazil, I promise you, my next flight will be out to see you in Seattle."

"I will hold you to that promise," said Cam.

They took a taxi a short distance to the high end glamorous club. A long line of people had formed at the club's entrance. Abrianna held Cameron's hand as they walked past people eager to get inside. Everyone noticed Abrianna and jumped forward to get a better view of her. In Italy, she had told Cam that she was a fashion model, but that was an understatement, she was a glamorous model. Abrianna smiled at the bouncer and said, "This is my boyfriend."

As the bouncer raised the rope allowing them to enter the club, a large black man who looked like a gangster with a diamond in his front tooth and a toothpick in his mouth reached out and grabbed Abrianna by her neck and said, "Honey, if you need a real man who can take care of you the way you want, I'm that man."

Cameron grabbed the man's fat pork chop hand and unwrapped the man's hand from Abrianna's neck and then struck him in the throat with such force that he collapsed on the ground. As the thug was falling, Cameron pulled two guns from his jacket, handed them to the bouncer, and said, "I don't think you want bad people in here."

Abrianna knew Cameron was a karate expert, having observed him teaching karate in Italy, but this rescue showed her what a special protector he would always be for her.

"What are your plans, Cam?" she asked as they sat comfortably at a head table near the front of the club's dance floor.

"I plan to get my college degree." "Cam, you are so smart and handsome."

She began to unbutton his shirt and his belt buckle. Slowly she slid her soft warm hands over his mightily muscled chest. Her hands got warmer. She closed her eyes to memorize every detail of his body.

Cam wanted to touch her. He really wanted her to know how much he wanted her. Beads of sweat formed on their foreheads. As her hands dove beneath his belt, the band started to play, "Get up and get Down," by the Dramatics. This was Big El's and Cam's party starter music in Italy. Couples had started to dance when Cameron decided to shake it on the dance floor. He looked into Abrianna's eyes and ripped off his shirt. A bouncer ran up to Cameron and told him to put on a shirt or he would have to leave. Abrianna walked over to her friend, the manager, who told Cameron, "One dance, then you will need a shirt." "Cameron's electric sexual dance steps made the women patrons stop their conversations. Cameron sizzled on the floor with his "twelve" pack stomach and body muscles. He added something new to his Philippine dance routine. It was a second, degree black belt dance to a kata few people had ever seen. He danced to the beat of the music and twisted his body to the beat of a karate master. His arms and hands signal a story of heated passion. Abrianna, the manager, the bouncer, and the patrons had never seen a sexier dance. When the music stopped, women ran up to Cameron and asked, "Where are you from? I love your eyes! Can I go home with you? Can I take you home? Do you have a twin brother?"

Cameron smiled. Abrianna was a tiny bit jealous, but said, "You are the most amazing man I have ever met. My love for you has soared even higher than in Italy." "I hate to say this but I need to go home."

"This is almost like Cinderella," said Cameron. "I feel like the prince and you are about to vanish." Abrianna hugged him and they walked to the subway nearest to her apartment. "Now be sure to count four stops and then get off the subway train. Your hotel will be across the street when you climb up the subway stairs."

Though it was cold, Cam's navy pea coat was very warm. Abrianna pressed Cam into her chest. Her lips warmed his soul. Cameron, "what will your parents say when they meet me?"

"They will say they love you."

"Well," said Abrianna, "I will be out there in no time. I love you."

Cameron walked down the subway stairs to catch the train.

Onboard the subway train, Cameron's mind revisited the evening with Abrianna. Though it seemed like a magical night, he understood two things: First, Gold Key No. 9 on love had not materialized. Second, he did not buy Abrianna's story about her roommate. Who was her roommate? After being away from your lover for months, wouldn't you tell your roommate to take a walk around the block or go on an errand? His mind then turned to Amy, whom he hoped to see in Canada the next day.

Cameron realized that his brain was in such a trance thinking about Abrianna and Amy that he forgot to count the train stops. He immediately jumped up, got off the train at the next stop, and walked up the subway steps to street level. He did not see the Hyatt or anything that looked familiar. He noticed how dark and eerie the street appeared. There were no cars, taxis, or trucks on the road. He did not know where he was; only several dimly lit lights illuminated the park, which looked like a huge graveyard with fog moving in slow motion. It was obvious he had missed his exit. He was lost. He walked back down the steps to the subway below hoping to catch a train to its next stop. Hopefully, someone on the train might know which exit he should take. Would there be a next train? It was getting late.

As Cameron waited for a subway train to arrive, he noticed five guys walking down the stairs about 600 feet to his left. He looked back at the stairs that he had just walked down and noticed another five guys wearing similar clothes coming down those steps. Instantly he realized these were really bad people. He could tell by their dress and swagger that they were coming to rob and possibly kill him. If he tried to jump and run down the subway tracks, they could block him. There was no other exit for him to escape. As the men raced toward him, he saw their knives and guns. He quickly looked the men over to see if the man he took down earlier in front of the club, with the diamond in his tooth, was a part of the gang. He wasn't there. Injury or death was imminent. The gang members raced to Cameron, the sounds of their footsteps growing louder and louder as they closed in on him.

He might take down one or two of the men, but going up against those guns looked to be a losing battle. Of all things, Cameron's mind shifted to a lesson his sensei had taught him approximately two years earlier, when he'd pointed to a man standing across the street and said, "Can you take him?"

"Yes, with one hand behind my back."

Sensei had not been pleased, as Cameron had underestimated his opponent, who was a 5th, degree black belt.

Back to the present he suddenly flipped up the collar of his pea coat and immediately went insane as the men were almost at an arm distance from him. He began jabbering incoherently, stuttering, and spitting. His mouth foamed a deep white froth with mucous flowing out of his nose. He punched the huge concrete column in front of him hard. He jabbered like a sick, punch-drunk boxer swearing and cursing. As fast as the gang was on top of him, they were gone. No damage to Cameron and no damage to the gangsters. Cameron had never gone to acting school, but he was certain his Black Belt instincts saved everyone. After all, who would want to lay a hand on a diseased man frothing at the mouth, swearing and kicking like a mad man who was possessed?

If he hadn't been so close to death, Cameron would have been laughing at how he overcome this deadly encounter with gang members. He also knew that this life, saving spiritual event was a sign that a Higher Being had plans for him.

Shortly, another train arrived, and Cameron took it to the next stop, where he eventually found his hotel.

The next morning, he caught a plane to Montreal. He had called Amy, who along with her best friend, Trista, were there to meet him at the airport. Amy's Nordic beauty was stunning, no doubt from her aerobic exercises, such as biking, running, and hiking. Tall blonde, buxom, and beautiful, Trista also looked absolutely adorable. They hugged and kissed.

Trista said, "So how is my sexy gay man, Big El?"

Cameron started tearing up about the lie he was about to tell. "Trista, Big El was killed in a horrible car accident two weeks ago in Greece.

Trista started screaming with bone chilling shrills.

"My God, this is horrible! He is, was, the only guy who didn't want my body. He just wanted to have fun. I love him, she moaned loudly." Trista went on, "When we get back to the apartment, I want to have a goodbye celebration of Big El's life. I want to make and light up paper boats and set them adrift with prayers like I have seen in Japan."

Montreal was a special city with architecturally unique buildings. He learned that the city had a population of over a million people who loved hockey. Hockey was more than a sport here, it was a religion. On an unfamiliar large lake, Trista set the paper boats adrift with lit candles, screaming, "Big El, I love you!" The boats moved through the water brightening the evening darkness.

Back at the apartment, Amy showed Cameron how much she loved him. Then Amy's door opened. It was Trista crying.

"Can I come in? I am so sad." Amy looked at Cameron and opened up the bedspread and sheets. What a wonderful evening Cameron had with two adorable Nordic Canadian beauties!

The next morning, Saturday, Cameron entertained the idea that maybe he should give up his thoughts of completing college, as he had found paradise in Montreal. The girls loved him. Yet, Golden Key No. 9 had not kicked in and he knew this was not real love, but it was a magnificent lust date. Amy and Trista were beautiful, sexy, and smart. Amy had a great job as an Administrative specialist with the Montreal City Government and Trista worked as an accountant at a nearby hospital. "Cameron, you don't have to work, we will take care of you," said Amy.

Maybe, I will stay for a while, he thought, laughing to himself.

That evening they had several drinks and laughed about the fun times in Italy and Switzerland with Big El.

"Cam, tomorrow is a special time at my family's house. Once a year Trista's family and my family get together for a big banquet, games, and lively conversation. I would love it if you would join us and meet our parents.

"Are you sure you want me to attend?"

"Yes Cam, they will love you and you will love them."

"Okay, when you put it like that, how can I refuse?"

The girls prepared a very nice breakfast for Cam with Canadian bacon, eggs, coffee cake, and Canadian coffee. They took him on a tour of Montreal, where they took turns kissing him at each tourist stop. How in the world could life get any sweeter than with two women who were the best of friends and who seemed to be in love with him?

They arrived at Amy's parents' house around noon. It was a rather wealthy looking large brick home in an exclusive suburb of the city. Cameron was introduced to Amy's and Trista's parents and the other twenty family members. As they were about to sit down at the dinner table, Amy's father said, "Cameron, I want to thank you for joining us for dinner so I can tell you that not only do I disapprove of you dating our daughter, I do not ever want you to see her again."

Cameron looked at Amy and Trista. They could not believe what they had heard.

"Father..." Amy started to say.

"Quiet, I am not done talking. I do not approve of any black man dating my daughter and I forbid you to ever see Amy again!"

This hatred was not new to Cameron, though he was surprised to hear it in Canada. He had heard that Canada was much more liberal than America. Hatred at Wilder College and by a preacher in high school was painful, but four years in the war, he had learned how he could personally beat racism. "Sir, you are making the biggest mistake of your life. Let me be clear, as a father, you want what is best for your daughter, but in this case you want what is best for you. I will tell you this sir, your daughter is 100 percent in love with me. I did not say 10 percent in love with me, I will repeat, she is 100 percent in love with me. So, If I leave as you are requesting, your daughter is going to hate you for the rest of your life. Do you understand me sir? If I walk out the door, your relationship with your daughter is over. Do you want that to happen?"

"Get out of this house!" he shouted.

Cameron nodded and walked to the door. The tension was unbearable. Cameron looked at the large bronze door knob, opened it, and never looked back.

The women followed him back to their apartment.

Amy and Trista were hysterically crying and tried to get Cameron to stay. He gathered his bags without saying a word and left.

He caught a plane to California to see Sharon, wondering if he was about to strike out with all three women. Sharon had broken Cameron's heart, had his baby, and left him for a married man with five children. He hoped to gather information on his baby. He had not seen or heard from her since he joined the Air Force. He wanted to see if the earth shook, rattled, and rolled, indicators of real love, when he saw her.

Sharon answered Cameron's telephone call and told him the restaurant where they could meet. Her words were nearly exactly as they had been four years earlier, when she dumped him. Even the restaurant looked similar, except it was more crowded.

"Hi, Cameron, it looks like the service was good to you. You really look toned up."

Nothing in his heart spoke to Cameron when he saw Sharon. "Thank you," said Cameron. "How have you been, Sharon?"

"I'm doing fine. I got my Master's Degree and my PhD," she responded.

"Are you married?" he asked?

"No, I divorced my first husband after he knocked out all my teeth and divorced my second husband, the stock broker, after he knocked out my false teeth. They both were very abusive and they knocked the hell out me. Luckily, I escaped with only my degrees to show for it."

"I am so sorry to hear what happened to you," said Cameron.

"What about you, Cameron?" she asked.

"I completed my military service and I intend to pursue my college degree," Cam replied.

"You my darling, should forget about a degree and concentrate on basket weaving. You are very buff and masculine, but I don't think college is for you," Sharon commented.

With the smallest spark of warmth burning for Sharon, any remaining passion for her quickly flamed out. To think that he carried that spark around the world facing horrific danger. She had now completely doused out the fire of love and that included friendship, "Have you heard anything about Morgan?" asked Cameron, referring to their son.

"No, not a word," she said.

"Goodbye Sharon, I don't anticipate we will ever see each other again."

Cameron did not try to hug her. He just walked out the restaurant just like he did four years ago, but this time, his heart was not broken.

Cameron arrived in Seattle and took a taxi to his mom's house. Along the way he noticed men with long ponytails. In the military, haircuts were short, so seeing men with ponytails and big Afros was new and unusual. He had seen men in New York and Montreal with long hair and now asked the taxicab driver about these new hair styles.

He said that the hippie movement was pretty much over and whatever remained had gone underground. Jobs exclusively in the preview of men, like butchers, bartenders, and maintenance individuals, were now performed by both women and men. Long hair for men of all races was in style.

Cameron's mother's house looked the same, maybe a little bit smaller due to the large Sequoia tree having grown for four years and was now taking over the front yard. He paid the taxicab driver and walked up to the door. The door was locked. His mother had never locked the door in all the years that she had lived in the house. What was going on? He rang the doorbell and his mother opened the door. Her voice was so filled with happiness as she said, "My son is home, my son is home from the war!" She gave him a wonderful motherly hug.

A young boy appeared near the door.

"Cameron this is your brother Benjamin. He's nearly ten years old. Benjamin, this is your big brother Cameron."

Benjamin was nearly six feet tall. Cameron remembered when he was a young baby with lots of wrinkly skin and he had nicknamed him Squiggly. He used to spin him around like a rag doll on one hand. His half-brother was going to be a big handsome young man. Benjamin would grow up to be nearly 6 feet 5 inches and 275 pounds and no more spins on Cameron's fingertips.

"Mom, how are my sisters?" asked Cameron.

"They're all doing fine. All three are married, all are nurses, all own houses, and they each live within five miles. They are all doing wonderfully. So tell me all about your military service," his mother asked.

"Did you get my letters?" asked Cameron.

"Yes, and I could certainly tell that my son was growing up to be a distinguished man in the service. I am so proud of you, Cam," she said.

"I was so fortunate, Mom," recalling his travels around the world. "I spent time in the Far East and visited countries throughout Europe. I had a wonderful time in the Philippine Islands, Switzerland, Greek Islands, and Italy. I especially enjoyed Rome, Florence, Venice, the Amalfi Coast, Sorrento, Pompeii, and Brindisi. Mom, I even had a villa on the Adriatic Ocean in the city of San Sabina. I can't wait for you to meet my good buddy, Big El. We started on the same day in the service and got out of the service on the same day. He lives in Rhode Island and is exceedingly smart, has a heart of gold, very funny, and is a great friend."

"One of the key things I learned, Mom, for a black man or any man who wants a chance to succeed in life, he must earn a college degree. So, I am going out to North University (NU) and see about enrolling."

"When I attend college, Mom, I will get the GI Bill, which as I understand will pay for my college expenses and a portion of the rent and food. I saved my money in the service and I hope to buy a car and not have to work while I attend classes."

"Oh Cam, thank you for the money that you sent home to us every month. We couldn't have made it without your support." She hugged Cameron. "Thank you, son, but now it's time for you to devote all your energy and money to the next phase of your life. You don't need to send me money. The girls are grown and moved out. My ex-husband sends money for Benjamin and me. Oh, your dad never did pay a dime of child support. Now I have met a man named Flint who I really like and he wants to get married and open up a restaurant. We will see if we can move forward on the restaurant idea. I've even picked out the restaurant's name, La Brindisi, from your travels in Italy. I think it's important now that your focus be on you and graduating from college. I love you, son!"

"Thank you, Mom. "When will I meet this man?"

"This weekend."

Cameron took several large boxes shipped from the Philippines and Italy downstairs to his mother's basement. When Cameron's sisters arrived a few days later, they walked directly downstairs and opened up the many gifts. It was like an early Christmas with carved wood statues and figurines, soup tureens, crystal wine glasses, and fine leather goods from Florence for them all.

Cameron got a ride with one of his sisters to his father's house. He managed to fit one of the wood boxes with gifts into the car. Everyone was very happy to see him. They loved the presents and were so thankful and pleased with Cameron's thoughtfulness. His stepmom said, "This calls for a shot of southern comfort." His dad, Dan, shook his hand. Cameron sensed his father's pride for completing four years of military service in the Air Force. He asked his father if he had visited with many of his old Tuskegee Airmen friends.

His father said, "Absolutely, many live in the Seattle area and we try to get together as often as we can. We have a bond that will no doubt continue forever!"

Cameron briefly told his dad about his military experience but really focused on his desire to start college. The last time his father had seen him, he'd been a broken man after flunking out of Wilder College.

"I think you are ready to start work in my real estate company," his Dad suggested.

"Thanks, Dad, but first I want to get my college diploma," Cam replied.

Cameron had matured beyond his father's expectation upon his return from the military. "Let's go hunting, son," his dad said.

"With ferrets, Dad?"

"No, we are going pheasant hunting with my trained dog named Lady," his Dad said.

"Who is this?" asked Cameron as he noticed a cute, reddish-brown dog. "This is Lady, my hunting dog," said Cameron's father, Dan. "She is a Vizsla, very affectionate, gentle, energetic, loyal, and an excellent pointer. I have taken my plane over to Eastern Washington where the birds are nice and fat from feeding on dry corn in the fields. Lady's a perfect hunting dog and with her point, I have shot many birds. Why don't you join me this weekend?"

"It sounds perfect, Dad. I bought a Remington 12-gauge shotgun in Italy and I've been dying to try it out."

Saturday came and Cameron was in his father's floatplane with Lady heading to the city of Umatilla, Oregon. He'd always loved to fly with his father. His father had been one of the greatest pilots in World War II. It was certainly difficult growing up with a war hero for a father, but his dad's daily battles in the skies fighting the enemy abroad and at the same time fighting racism in the military, had equipped his powerful father to help guide Cam through many difficult situations in the Air Force.

They landed on a nearby lake, and hiked about a mile until they reached a large farm with corn stalk drying in the fields. The farmer gave them permission to hunt on his land.

Dad had trained Lady well, as she pointed to the pheasants that were hiding beneath fallen corn stalks. Lady had a beautiful sleek auburn coat and obeyed Dan's every command. What a glorious day, thought Cameron. The sun shone brightly in the sky. It was perfect hunting weather. Most of the corn had been harvested, but lying on the ground were stalks, leaves, husks, and cobs which still had many kernels of corn which the pheasants gobbled up like candy. The fallen corn stalk had a wonderful pungent aroma. Almost like smelling an expensive glass of Bordeaux wine. Lady eagerly walked the field, looking back at us as if to signal, "I am over here!" Suddenly, her body froze and her nose pointed to something in the stalks of corn. "Get them, Lady!" Lady charged the pheasants, who immediately took flight. The male ring-necked pheasants were absolutely beautiful with colors of red, and green, and a white collar. They were easy to differentiate from the females, who were several shades of brown.

At a loud blow of Dan's whistle, Lady lurched at the bird hidden in the corn field. The pheasant raced to fly away. Dan, with his Browning automatic shotgun, used one shot to knock the bird out of the sky. Seconds later, another bird took to the air and Cameron blasted away at the bird with his new Remington shotgun. It took two shots, but he got his first pheasant. Minutes later, Lady sprung a third and then a fourth bird. Within an hour Cameron and his father had reached their bag limit of pheasants. Lady was an excellent pheasant hunting dog. Tired, with her tongue hanging low in her mouth, she basked in the hugs and petting she received.

Cameron's stepmother was so pleased to see all the pheasants that they brought back. She took two pheasants, feathered and cleaned them, and poured orange juice over them and let them marinate for about two hours. She then wrapped them in bacon and added salt and pepper and then baked them slowly along with wild rice. The quality and delicious taste of pheasant was really enjoyable to Cameron. Pheasant under glass is a meal fit for a king.

He especially enjoyed his time hunting with his dad. Following this trip Cameron made it a point to join his dad at least two or three times a year for pheasant hunting in Eastern Washington. Dan always flew his plane on each pheasant hunt.

The next day, Cameron met his mother's future husband, Flint, a retired marine serviceman. In many ways, he felt sorry for Flint as there was absolutely no way for him to replace his father. But as long as he made his Mom happy, Cameron was happy.

Several days later, Cameron went to visit his grandmother Priscilla on his dad's side.

"Grandma, I really missed you while I was traveling the world serving in the Air Force. How have you been?" he asked.

"I've been fine, Cameron, just getting up there in age, but I'm doing fine," she replied.

"How are my aunt and uncles doing?" he inquired.

"Your Aunt Carol has been working for a huge corporation where she is an executive secretary for a senior vice president. I hear she's making a lot of money and loves her job. She is very talented and I am so happy for her. Oh, your aunt Carol is still married to Walter. He works on vintage cars and boats. I heard he recently restored a luxury Chris Craft wooden boat."

"Your uncle Warren is on administrative leave for being the first black police officer to shoot a white criminal." Warren was the third oldest in the family. He was very light-skinned and he looked almost white. On one unfortunate day, he shot and killed a white person who was in the process of committing a felony. Shortly thereafter he discovered that it didn't matter how white your skin looked. If you were black and killed a white person, everyone hated you. Society would not tolerate black men killing white men. He had one son and three daughters. "He's not too happy with the backlash and the lack of support from his fellow officers and community. I don't know what is going to happen to him, because he is not very happy."

"Your uncle David is a gifted electrician. He's currently working on a state-of-the-art project for a major aviation corporation. David was the youngest of Dan's siblings. He was a star sprinter in high school and went on to work for a large public works company where he was instrumental in developing state-of-the-art transportation networks. He had three sons and three daughters."

"Grandma, when dad and I served in the military, we fought for freedom for all citizens. How have race relationships progressed over the past four years?" Cam asked.

"While I can't speak for other parts of the country, here in Tacoma and Seattle it has not been good," she replied.

"Why grandma?" asked Cameron.

"Most of the hatred towards blacks is no longer as easily transparent. It has gone underground in many respects. First of all, your dad and uncles will tell you, banks make it exceedingly difficult for blacks to buy houses and gain the basic building block for economic wealth. For example, the banks have adopted a practice called red-lining. They basically have drawn a red line around the central area of Seattle and won't loan money in that area where the majority of citizens are black. It doesn't matter how much income one has. If you are black and live in this area the banks won't loan to you. Now piggyback that with the lack of education for blacks in Seattle. Fewer and fewer blacks are graduating from high school and going to college. Whites are moving to the suburbs leaving many vacant homes that are now decaying. With so many jobless blacks, they are relegated to trying to make a living by selling drugs. Many blacks in this climate of drug sales have been caught and have been sentenced to long prison terms. The climate for blacks is deplorable and hostile. It is the modern-day version of slavery, something your great-grandmother tried to escape, when she left Marshall, Texas over sixty-five years ago."

"How is great-grandma?" asked Cameron.

"She's fine and will be turning 100 soon. I'll let you know when we have her birthday party."

"Grandma," said Cameron, "I believe education is the key to economic prosperity and I intend to go back to college and earn my degree. When I was in the service, I met many brilliant men but most did not have a college degree and their opportunity for higher rank was very limited."

"Wonderful Cameron. I know you will be successful!"

"Thanks, Grandma. It was great seeing you. I promise to keep you up to date on my progress through college."

Following his father's military service as a Tuskegee airman, Dan had established himself as a very successful real estate broker. At one point he owned over 100 houses. Dan was wealthy at one point but it all came to an end during the Boeing bust in the 1960s and '70s when people were saying "Will the last person to leave Seattle turn out the lights." Nearly all of Dan's houses had three to four bedrooms. He was highly leveraged on all the houses. When the laid-off Boeing employees could no longer pay rent, he could no longer pay the mortgages, and he lost all the houses, except his home and one rental.

Cam now made it a point to visit with his mother's brothers and sisters to see how they were doing.

His mother's oldest brother, Paige Jr., had traveled with Cameron's grandfather from Omaha, Nebraska to Seattle in search of work at the beginning of World War II. He eventually joined the army and was shipped overseas where he fought in the Philippines. He sent money home to his father to help the family. Eventually he married and had six children and became a very wealthy real estate broker.

Next was Uncle Thas who became a merchant seaman during the war and then a longshoreman. Eventually he married twice and had four children. He was an extremely handsome man and his children could've been in a high-fashion magazine for their stunningly handsome and gorgeous features.

Cameron's Uncle Wyman was a college-educated mathematician and opera singer. Although he was close to graduating, he never graduated due to a lack of funds. He was exceedingly smart and had an operatic voice that inspired listeners.

Then there was his Aunt Vine. She was a beautiful TV star who married a famous singer. One of his songs made it to number one on the hit parade. They had two gifted children who wrote songs for famous Hollywood singers.

Uncle Lionist was the first to graduate from college. He became a First Lieutenant in the army. He was an excellent skier and had taught Cameron how to do jumps and flips on skis. He had even made a pair of wood skis for Cameron. He married a very beautiful lady and Cameron served in their wedding. Tragically his life was cut short while serving on military duty. They did not have any children.

Next was Uncle General as he liked to be called. He had a wonderful smile and a great sense of humor. America wasn't ready for a black movie star when the General came along. He was handsome with straight jet-black hair and a Clark Gable-like mustache. He had perfect diction. Cameron remembered seeing the reaction of ladies that were introduced to him. It was all smiles. He married a lovely artist and they had three children.

Aunt Olive was the youngest of the children. Everyone wanted to spoil her. She was full of love, laughter, and happiness. It was no surprise that when she grew up with love all around her, she became an ordained minister. She met and married an inspiring man and they had three gifted children.

All the aunts and uncles were pleased to see Cameron. They each painted a difficult economic climate for blacks. Cameron reiterated that he didn't want to be a statistic so he would be attending college and he would obtain a degree.

Cameron decided to call his uncle Walter to see if he could help him find a nice used car.

His uncle said, "Sure I would be happy to do that and welcome back from the service."

They went to several car dealerships and looked at many cars. Then they found a 1967 Firebird 400.

"My God," said uncle Walter. "This has to be the fastest car in Seattle. Probably not appropriate for a college student."

Cameron had never seen a street car that shot fire out of its rear end as the front end of the car raised one to three feet off the ground. While test driving the car, it roared like thunder as it proceeded down the highway. Cameron could easily handle the steering wheel, but it took practice shifting the powerful transmission as the car raced down the road like it was a contender in the Daytona 500.

Walter laughed. "This car is in perfect shape mechanically but the gas bill alone is going to be very expensive."

He was so right, as Cameron could literally see the gas gauge fall when he gunned the engine hard. "Cameron, you don't need to race any cars, including Corvettes, because this car will take anything that is street legal."

Cameron fell in love with the car and paid cash for it. He thanked his uncle for helping him find his dream car. The car needed new rims and wheels and a significant amount of detailing. Cameron laughed to himself as he now had the fastest car in Seattle but he had to drive slowly so as not to attract the police. Heads would often turn when they looked at his finely tuned muscle car.

Cameron rocked in his newly purchased purple Firebird 400 as he drove down the city streets. *Purple Haze*, by Jimi Hendrix played on the radio. Cameron loved the song, having purchased a copy of it while in the Philippines. Cameron thought it was a prophecy song, as it spoke to him on the calamity of the Vietnam war, love, peace, drugs, freedom, and death, maybe even Jimi's death. Cameron was so mesmerized by the lyrics that he went to the library to learn more about Jimi Hendrix. According to his research, Jimi was born on November 27, 1942 and died in London September 18, 1970. He was buried in the Greenwood Cemetery in Renton, Washington. Interestingly, Jimi's parents had met in the same way as Cameron's parents, at a dance in Seattle. Another interesting fact was that one of Jimi's first songs was the theme from Peter Gun which was so popular with Cameron's high school classmates.

Cameron had one more stop to make before applying to NU. He drove his hot rod over to visit his old grade, middle, and high school buddy, Nelson. Nelson was now sporting glasses, his brown hair more blonde and receding.

He was really happy to see Cameron. Cameron learned that Nelson's father had died shortly after he left to join the air force. "He really liked you," said Nelson. "He knew if anybody could catch Ole' fighter it would be you." For years, Ole' fighter had tugged and broken many fishing lines off Nelson's dock. No one could catch it. One grand day, in the presence of Nelson's father, Cameron caught the thirty-five-pound carp.

His mother still lived in the waterfront home on Lake Washington. Nelson had completed four years of pre-med school at NU. He hoped to become a doctor in three to four more years. He had married a very smart and lovely Chinese lady named Irene. She was an accountant working in a large accounting firm in Seattle.

After everyone had caught up on what they had been up to, Cameron mentioned to Irene that he heard she was an expert reader of Tarot cards.

She told him that her parents taught her how to read Tarot cards long ago when she was a teenager and asked if Cam would like to have a reading? Cam really did not believe in the black magic of these cards but, ever since the Ouija board warning to Big El in Italy that correctly came to pass, he'd thought it might be interesting to see what these cards might have to say about his future.

"Irene, do you mind giving me a prediction on whether or not I will ever graduate from undergraduate school?"

"I would be happy to," said Irene. Unlike most fortune tellers who keep their cards close by, Irene returned from her den down the hall and showed Cam a beautifully polished smooth wood box. Inside was an ornately decorated silk cloth bag that contained cards unlike any cards he had ever seen.

"Cameron, I want you to cut the cards."

Moments later, after she had arranged the cards, she said, "according to these cards, Cameron, you are not only going to graduate from undergraduate school, but you are going to go much further."

"Are you certain?" Cameron asked optimistically.

"Absolutely," she replied.

"Will you do me another favor?" asked Cameron. "I'd like to get a little more feedback from the tarot cards. I like to calibrate the cards for accuracy. Would you mind telling me how many years you and Nelson will be married?"

"Cam, I never do my own readings, but I will humor you this time," Irene said.

After shuffling the cards, she turned over a card that had absolutely zero meaning to Cameron. Her face turned ghoulishly flush and she immediately put away the cards.

"What's the matter?" asked Cameron.

"Nothing," said Irene, "I just do not do my own readings."

Cameron had received a phone call from a NU counselor telling him he had been accepted into the university and when to report for classes.

Now the only thing left on his to-do list was to find an apartment close to the university. The first apartment he looked at was elegant and very expensive. It was located on the shores of Lake Washington. He knocked on the apartment manager's office door. He told the lady that he was interested in renting an apartment. She looked at him and said she was sorry but there were no vacancies and she had meant to take the sign down. Cameron did not believe her for a second. He looked her squarely in the eyes and said, "Did I just return from a battle abroad to give you the right to reject my right to rent one of your apartments based on the color of my skin?"

"I'm sorry," she said.

Cameron continued his search for an apartment. He came across a very nice apartment building about a mile from the university, which came with a heated swimming pool.

Cameron stood facing the manager of this apartment and said, "All I want is a small apartment so I can attend college to see if I can graduate. I have the money. I am a veteran. I am a good American, I just need an apartment."

The manager started to say no, when his wife interrupted and said, "Can we call you back this afternoon?"

"Yes, of course," Cameron responded.

The manager called back two hours later and apologized for his initial rejection. "I also served in Vietnam and I am going to school. Your message really hit home with me. You, Cameron, have yourself an apartment. When can you move in?"

Cameron said, "Today." The manager and his wife would soon become dear friends of Cameron.

# Chapter 2

# Big El

Big El was raised watching Abbott and Costello, Jerry Lewis and Dean Martin movies. His father gave him a big box of popcorn each evening as he watched a new movie. Big El, knew that someday he might be a comedian. Even Cameron said that he was better than Don Rickles and Johnny Carson.

Big El's first job after the Air Force was working a for a friend who was an emergency room doctor. Dr. Avner handled trauma and emergency conditions such as bullet and knife wounds for Charter Oak Hospital. He was on call twenty-four hours a day. The hospital was experiencing an epidemic of shootings, broken bones, heart attacks, car accident traumas, and burns. The emergency room was a very challenging place to work with deaths occurring daily. Dr. Avner needed another volunteer and a staff member to assist him in the emergency room.

So here was Big El lying flat on his back, lying on a metal gurney, wearing nothing but a hospital gown. He laughed out loud as he propelled himself from one wall to another with his exploding farts. He was amazed at how loud he could make the metal gurney ring in the sterile room and how fast he could make the gurney travel. There was no activity, a rare moment in the emergency room. Eventually, Big El reached the elevator door and he pushed the up button. He propelled the gurney like a motor scooter onto the elevator. As the door closed, he proceeded to blow farts like a conductor in a famous bass symphony. His smile grew louder. Four floors up, three nurses entered the elevator and the door closed quickly. The nurses gasped for air and said, "Oh, my God! Big El was so embarrassed. He said, "I am so sorry, I feasted on fried bats last night and those critters keep flying out of me."

Eventually, the hospital hired Big El at minimum wage to assist Dr. Avner and the nurses, with clerical and basic clinical tasks for incoming patients.

Big El was happy with how things were starting out in his non-military service life. Although he missed all the activities with his service buddies, especially Cameron, he was now with Susan, whom he loved so much. With every flower he placed beside Susan's dinner plate, every passionate kiss she gave him, he knew that he was with the most beautiful, loving, and marvelous woman in the world. He once told Cameron that Susan was much more than a soulmate. She was his universe.

What Big El needed now was to find a better paying job so he could marry Susan. He considered his options and came up with three:

First, he could return to college using his G.I. Bill. He figured that he needed to complete three and a half years of school. College graduates were not making huge sums of money at the time so he crossed off going back to college.

Second, the University of Rhode Island was still offering him a full baseball scholarship. The thought of how statistically remote his chances were of making the big leagues and the months away from Susan were a deciding factor, so he crossed the training to become a professional baseball player off his list.

Third, there was the State Patrol. Baroni, his old family friend, encouraged him to join the Rhode Island State Patrol. Big El loved this goal because he would be helping people and it would provide very nice benefits, so he could marry Susan and spend the rest of his life in her arms. There was only one problem. It was hard to get into the academy. This was what he wanted. Big El's career goal of becoming a state trooper was now in focus.

One evening at the hospital with patients lined up in the hallways, Dr. Avner told Big El, "Take this needle and thread and stitch this patient up now! We do not have one additional hand and I'm working on another patient. Can you do that for me?"

"Absolutely," said Big El. "Are you going to give him any pain killer," asked Big El?

"We don't have time," said Dr. Avner.

Big El washed his hands. He had zero training on how to put stitches in somebody's body but he remembered darning a sock once. As the needle was inserted into the patient's knee, with no pain medicine, the screams got louder and louder forcing Big El to complete the task quickly.

"Great job" said Dr. Avner.

"Just call me Dr. Big El," he said, with a grin on his face.

Shortly thereafter Big El got a job with the police department for the city of Gloucester, Rhode Island. After cadet training he teamed up with a veteran police officer. When they came on duty, they were assigned neighborhoods to patrol for DUIs, speeders, and other crimes. Big El was issued a handgun, a wooden baton, and a flashlight. He had extensive training as a cadet on the use of his handgun plus he was an ace marksman stemming from his military days. Months into his training, he was given his own squad car and given specific neighborhoods to patrol alone.

He confided to Cameron that he was certain that he ticked off that police department because he didn't write many tickets. Unless a driver was hitting other cars or speeding 20 to 30 miles over the speed limit he did not issue a ticket. He would pull the driver over and make them take a taxi home. He knew how difficult it was for people to make money and then have to pay hefty fines, so he gave sound but hard advice to many offenders in the town.

Big El was surprised to hear that he had received several letters of praise from residents of the city of Gloucester. A judge and a priest topped the list.

These letters made it impossible for the police Captain to fire his rookie policeman.

In June, Big El received a letter stating that he had been accepted into the Rhode Island State Police Academy. It was his dream come true. Even though he had received some support from many friends and relatives, Big El had earned acceptance into the academy on his own. No one pulled any strings to help him get in. He had one mentor, Baroni, who encouraged him, but he earned entrance on his own. His classes would start in January.

At the academy he scored high, and received the highest marksmanship scores ever achieved with a revolver, near-perfect classroom test scores, and he was well liked.

To be sure, Big El was funny, witty, and a jokester at heart. His years of watching Abbott and Costello, Dean Martin and Jerry Lewis, and other comic movies during his dad's second job at the downtown movie theater made it second nature for him to make people laugh which he loved. His instructors and fellow cadets also saw his brilliantly serious side when the occasion arose. Big El climbed to the head of his class. No one doubted that he had what it took to one day lead the men in the Rhode Island State Patrol in their navy-blue uniforms, with red stripes, and tan hats.

Big El had a huge smile when he graduated from the academy. Susan, looked at Big El in his trooper's uniform and said, "My you are such a good-looking man with your blonde locks of hair, blue eyes, rugged muscular German build, and big leather boots. I have a good strong man."

It was now spring of 1973. Big El had just rented a beautiful two-bedroom modern brick condo with a large heated swimming pool. Susan moved in with him. He laughed often and remarked, "You are the best roommate I've ever had."

# Chapter 3

# Cameron's College Years

C ameron parked his car on the first day of his colleges classes in the parking lot where puddles of water had formed. He looked up towards the University and noticed the gray clouds and the big canopy of trees with their foliage of beautiful red, yellow, and green leaves. The leaves were falling and blowing in the wind on this chilly autumn morning.

Cameron took a deep breath. From a .5 GPA to gold key numbers two and three: You can achieve anything you desire, it just depends on how hard are you willing to work for it. Go to college.

This was it, this was his new battle, there was no turning back. This was it!

Cameron followed many other students up the 2,000-step pathway to the buildings on top of the hill. He eventually located his curriculum advisor's office.

Cameron had been accepted into the University based on his high school GPA and his national merit scores, and definitely not his GPA at Wilder.

"Good morning Mr. Price," said the advisor. "I have some good news for you. The University has elected to give you credit for the one and a half years you attended Wilder College. Wilder College has a reputation for high academics and while you received a .5 GPA, the University believes that would've translated into a higher GPA here.

This means that we will not put you on academic probation and you are 2 1/2 years from completing your degree."

This was spectacular news, " Thank you very much," Cameron responded.

"Now, Mr. Price, here is your first quarter's class schedule," said his advisor.

Cameron noticed the advisor never looked him in the eyes and tended to glance to his lower left when he talked to him. This was a sign of racial hatred that he had come to detect. He looked at his class schedule and instantly knew the advisor had set him up for failure: calculus, economics, statistics, organic chemistry, and physics. "No way," said Cameron. "I am not going to take this heavy a class load."

"Yes you are," said his advisor. "That is what I've scheduled you for, especially given your late admission into the University and the availability of classes."

"Sir, thank you for accepting my admission into the university, but listen to me closely. I have been away from the academic university setting serving our country in the military overseas for nearly four years. I am going to take easier classes so I have more time to better adjust to classroom expectations. So I am going to outline the following classes that I would like to take and you will not stand in my way. I'm going to take speech I, music appreciation, political science, and wealth accumulation.

"No way, I cannot approve those classes."

"Are you paying for me to take classes at NU?" Cameron asked. "Why can't I take the classes that I want to take and those that I'm paying for? Let me make it crystal clear to you sir, after I get written approval from each professor teaching those classes that I want to take, I will be back. If you don't approve my classes, I promise you that my very next discussion will be in front of the local TV stations. I don't think that the public would like to know how you propose to set up a returning black military veteran for failure."

Cameron left the counselor's office and embarked on a signature-gathering campaign. In less than an hour, Cameron had received signatures from all the professors on his list inviting him to attend their classes.

His counselor saw all the signatures and to Cameron's amazement he approved the revised courses.

Cameron walked daily to his classes up the 2,000-step pathway corridors to the University's classrooms. He was motivated and focused like never before, putting in hours and hours of studying on each and every subject. He stayed up late each night practicing and practicing his speeches and other classroom homework. Eventually, he gathered enough courage to consistently raise his hand in class to answer the professor's questions. He had no social life as he studied nearly every minute that he was awake.

His mid-quarter grades were all A's.

On several occasions as he climbed the steps, he ran into fellow students. One was a cute blonde named Laura and then there was an adorable brunette named Polly. Cameron learned that Laura was from Idaho and wanted to get a psychology degree and Polly was from Eastern Washington and wanted to get an English degree. They chatted along the way. Laura mentioned that she had been married and her ex-spouse was now in prison for ten years on an assault conviction. He thought it was strange that she would tell him about her personal life after only walking a few flights of stairs. To be clear, Cameron was 100 percent focused on his college coursework and not the ladies, until he met Chaplin.

Chaplin was a male friend of Nelson's, who was also attending NU. He was majoring in psychology. Chaplin came by Cameron's apartment occasionally on Saturday nights and the two would go out to several nearby clubs. After the fourth Saturday, they developed a routine that went like this: Cameron played several Smokey Robinson records on his stereo while they both drank a shot of Johnny Walker. After the third song, they were fired up and ready to have fun at the clubs and they did.

On Sunday, Cameron was back studying.

One evening Cameron received a telephone call in his apartment. When he picked up the phone and said hello, no one answered. He could hear that someone was on the phone and the person was breathing deeply and loudly. Cameron had never received an obscene phone call and he hung up. The calls persisted. Cameron had no idea who was calling him. He could not tell if the breathing was from a guy or gal. Nearly two months passed by with more calls of heavy panting. Then one Sunday evening, the phone rang again and the deep breathing started. This time, Cameron did not hang up the phone but said in Spanish, "Como se Llama?"

The caller, believing she had called the wrong number said, "Oh I am so sorry. I obviously misdialed." Cameron immediately recognized the voice. It was Laura, his stair-walking friend.

"Laura, why have you been hounding me with your deep-breathing phone calls?"

She hung up and Cameron never received another phone call from her again nor did he ever see her on the steps to his classes.

Cameron's first-quarter grades were in his apartment mailbox. He picked up his report card and slowly, very slowly opened it. He glanced down at the cumulative GPA. It read 4.0. He was shocked beyond belief. He was ecstatic. He did a little happy dance by his mail box, and wished that he could have been finished with college that very moment, however this was just the beginning.

He returned for a meeting with his curriculum advisor.

The advisor, never looking at Cameron, seemed hell-bent on ensuring that Cameron flunked out of the university. He again assigned him challenging courses. "Cameron, you want to get into the business school and the only way you can do it is by getting good grades in calculus, micro and macro economics, plus statistics. You can only take one economics course this quarter so that means that you'll have to wait another quarter to get into the business school."

"Okay," said Cameron, "If you can assign me this insane workload this quarter then I'm going to take both economic courses so I can start business school next quarter."

"You can't do it, Cameron."

Well, here's my 4.0 GPA report card and I will do it.

The advisor seemed overly pleased to sign off on Cameron's quarterly courses.

It was now Cameron's do or die moment. He had to pass all the courses to get into business school or his dream of graduating from college was over.

When Cameron came back to his apartment, he received a call from Big El. "Hey buddy, any Camels out your way?" Camel was short for Cameron and Big El. When the names were combined, it meant that they could never be beat.

"Dang straight," replied Cam. "How are you, buddy?"

"I had to pull a Camel nearly daily to get a job on the local police force," said Big El. My friend Baroni says that he can get me a job with the state police here in Rhode Island in about a year, maybe less, if I do well here. I have been attending police training school nearly every day learning the ropes. They are so serious over there. I had to cut down on partying and drinking so I could pass successive tests. There isn't a day that goes by that I don't think of all the fun we had. Cam, I just look forward to crossing this next hurdle so we can get back together."

"How's Susan?" Cam inquired.

"She is so understanding, passionate, and loving. I'm so lucky. That's why I called you, Cam. I'm a really lucky guy to have her and I am going to ask her to marry me. Susan my fiancée, doesn't that have a nice ring to it? Speaking of rings, I hocked every asset I have to buy her a big ring and I'm talking a massively enormous diamond ring."

"Sounds like you may have to work overtime or take on a second job to pay for that ring," Cam suggested.

"Great minds think alike! That's exactly what I had to do to afford the ring that I want to buy her. I am working all the overtime I can get."

"Hey buddy," said Cameron, "call me after you ask Susan to marry you. I want to hear every detail. Congratulations!"

"How's Abrianna?" asked Big El. "Did you see her after you left us?"

"She was more beautiful than ever. She said to say hello to you with a warm hug from her."

"Dang Cam, She is so fine."

"It's funny that you mentioned her as I was thinking about calling her and inviting her to come out to see me."

Cameron then told Big EL about seeing the girls in Canada. "Big El, why did you make me tell Trista that you were dead? I felt so weird listening to her agonizing screams of pain and her candles floating on water to wish you a bon voyage to heaven."

"Hey, I really appreciate it. Thanks. I actually no longer feel her spirit close to me which makes it so much easier to ask Susan to be my wife. You know, I never did a thing with that girl but she wanted me in the worst way and I just wanted to have fun. I think she must be skilled in dark magic as she had a spell on me."

Cameron then told Big El about Amy's father. The trip to paradise had turned into a disastrous journey through bigot land.

He also told Big El that he'd met with his old girlfriend Sharon and it was 100 percent, make that 200 percent over.

"You will find Ms. Right, Cam," said Big El.

Back on campus, Cameron ran up each of the 2,000 steps carrying a full backpack of textbooks. Things were going well until he sat down to start his calculus class. He looked around the large classroom filled with nervous students. The professor walked into the class and placed his lecture notes on the lectern. He said, "Ladies and gentlemen, welcome to calculus I. To pass my class you will need a thorough understanding of the theorems of calculus, derivatives, antiderivatives, integrals, sine, cosine, tangent, and velocity." As the professor continued, Cameron's eyes dazed into a thick gray fog as he didn't understand one word. He was totally lost by the time the professor talked briefly about the wrapping formula. In less than three minutes, Cameron felt his college career slipping away. He stood up and walked out of the room. There was no point in wasting time if he was going to fail calculus. As he walked to his car, he wondered what he would do for the rest of his life. He was really sad. In spite of a 4.0 point GPA last quarter, a stellar military career as perhaps one of the nation's great spies, he had failed. His father and all the other Tuskegee Airmen had received college degrees and Cameron apparently did not have the mental skills to pass calculus. He thought about Gold Key No. 3, get a college degree or go to prison. He now awaited a not so bright future. Then he thought about Gold Key No. 2, you can achieve anything you desire if you are prepared to work for it. Last, he thought about Irene and her tarot card prediction. His agony was building as he continued to walk farther from the calculus class. He wondered what life could have been, had he not encountered bitter racism at Wilder University and received his degree there. Calculus on the other hand was an equal opportunity class meaning either you get it right or you get it wrong, but there was no gray area for racism. Cameron pondered whether calculus was indeed necessary for a business degree or if it was adopted to hinder women and minorities from being admitted into the business school. Nothing mattered now, as it was over.

Cameron walked past the last building before the pathway down to his car. He noticed a very small sign near one of the windows on that building. It barely caught his attention. He stopped and walked back to that sign. It read "tutor services for students in need of class room assistance. Cameron needed a tutor!

Cameron walked inside the building and asked the receptionist if they had a calculus tutor.

"Yes. Darlene Thomas is our calculus tutor. She's in now. Would you like to meet her?"

"Absolutely," said Cameron.

Shortly, Darlene walked up to Cameron. This woman was so beautiful that Cameron thought she must be Darlene's assistant. She was drop dead gorgeous.

"Hi, I am Darlene and I understand you would like some assistance with calculus." She spoke very professionally and stayed on the subject of calculus. "Cameron, calculus is really easy and if you allow me, I will help you break it down."

"I'm all yours. When can we get started?" asked Cameron, trying to fight his urge to flirt with her. She was a tall brunette and very sexy.

"Let's start tomorrow and then we should meet each morning before your calculus class."

Cameron had never had a tutor before. Now he had one of the smartest and most beautiful lady who could help him pass calculus.

"Oh, I forgot to ask you," said Cameron, "do you charge by the hour or by the quarter?"

"Neither," said Darlene. "NU is paying my salary as they have learned that a large pocket of the student body requires assistance with calculus and other courses."

The next day was the first tutoring session. Darlene said, "Cameron, stand up."

Cameron stood up.

"Now shake your entire body really hard. What you are doing is shaking off the misconception that you may have about calculus." Darlene then continued her lesson explaining the elementary principles of calculus. She made calculus seem easy.

Cameron's smile soon returned. He was finally understanding calculus. Each session was more beneficial as he could speak and write calculus formulas. Soon, he became the first person in the class to raise his hand and answer the professor's questions.

Cameron's positive classroom energy spilled over into all of his other classes. He threw himself into all of his homework assignments including microeconomics and macroeconomics, with more than average enthusiasm, and found himself in the library not only studying the weekly assignments but preparing for the next weekly study assignments. The library became his new home. He was a natural in his statistics class when the professor asked what was the probability of a flipped penny landing on heads.

"Fifty percent."

"You sir, are correct," said the professor. The professor smiled as he immediately shifted to what Cameron called tough statistics. Specifically, when to use and apply the empirical rule to help you decide whether a sample of data came from a normal distribution. Statistics appeared to be an excellent tool for forecasting voter approval and disapproval, and other probable outcomes, but Cameron decided to use it to personally help him from that day forward. Then the light bulb came on. College courses were simple tools to help him expand his accomplishments at work, at home, and along the journey of life. This realization was key to Cameron's newfound interest in his classes.

Each day Cameron beamed with enthusiasm and he thanked Darlene for her tutoring sessions. The seeds of learning had sprouted and he was growing in the right direction.

Cameron elected to turn out for spring football. He visited the dean of the law school to obtain a legal opinion on how much football eligibility he had after playing one year at Wilder College.

He was disappointed when he learned that he only had one year remaining. He thought the dean had made a mistake and asked him to review his decision.

"Sorry," he said, "only one year left."

Well, one year was better than none. He loved football so he tried out. He lifted heavy weights in the large weight room with the other football players. He thought it was odd that none of the players in the gym laughed and none of players inspired others to lift heavier weights. Cameron ran 10 miles every day including running up and down the stadium steps and the 2,000 steps from the parking lot.

In the evening, before he settled down to do his homework, Cameron taught karate class for minority youth in central district of Seattle. Cameron enjoyed showing his students basic Karate skills. They in turn were mesmerized each time Cameron went through his katas, which were precision blocks, kicks and punches.

The combination of football and karate conditioning resulted in huge biceps, shoulder, leg, neck muscles and amazingly fast speed. During time trials, Cameron learned that he was the second-fastest player on the team. He was second only to the quarterback. Normally running backs were the fastest. Cameron had blazing speed, perfect for a wide receiver.

When his second quarter came to an end, he received the following grades: A+ in calculus (the highest grade in his class), A's in microeconomics and macroeconomics, and an A in statistics. Cameron had received a 4.0+.

He walked over to Darlene's to show his grades. How lucky he was to see that little sign on the building. How lucky he was to have Darlene as a tutor. Was it luck? Was it divine intervention? Was it both?

Darlene, "here are my grades."

"Very nice, Cameron, very nice," she said.

"May I hug you?" asked Cameron.

"Of course," she said.

Cameron hugged her. It was a nice, but there was no spark. It wasn't a love hug. It wasn't a sad hug even though he knew he may never see her again, it was a genuine thank you hug for without her help he would never have been able to get into business school. "Thank you," he said with a tear of appreciation forming in his eye.

Cameron was thrilled. He had now been formally accepted into the business school. His parents were overjoyed to hear the news.

He picked up the phone and called Big El. "Hey buddy, what's going on?"

"I found that two-carat diamond ring for Susan. It's huge and very expensive. I didn't even have to reach out to the Mafia for assistance this time. I paid every penny of it myself."

"Have you picked a day yet?" asked Cameron.

"No, I'm going to ask her in about three months," replied Big El. "Baroni is encouraging me to get that state patrol job and I think that will be a perfect time to start our new life together."

"Awesome Big El," said Cameron.

Cam updated him on his endeavors with football, karate, and his progress through his university courses.

"Man, I wish I were there with my bola bag and toilet plunger to cheer your team on," said Big El with a laugh.

"So what's up with Abrianna?"

"She called and sent me several letters. She plans to come to Seattle this weekend, now that the toughest courses are behind me. I think she will be here for about a week."

"Good luck. You are the only guy I know that is dating a New York high-fashion model. She's extremely foxy, you lucky dog."

"Hey," Big El inquired, "Have you heard from any of our friends from the service?"

"Yeah," said Cam. "Our pal Art, who became a sexual conquest of a passionate cougar senorita in Acuna, Mexico, married Susie. They have a baby boy and live in Baltimore. I wonder if he will bring all of Susie's family to the United States."

"Maxwell married his high school sweetheart. No kids yet, but I heard that he is working as a mechanic in an auto repair shop. He told me that when I talked to you, to be sure and tell you that when I stabbed him in the hand, it was the best thing that ever happened to him. He got out of the service during Vietnam and he ended up marrying his dream girl. Big El, when I accidentally stabbed Maxwell, it really shook me up. Can you imagine putting a knife clean through one of your good friend's hands?" said Cameron.

"I got a card from one of my Philippine service friends who you never met. I called him GW for his passion for golf and women. He got a job as a warehouseman in Southern California. He said he was thinking about going back to college and had recently been accepted at Ohio State University. He still plays golf and said his poker game has picked up tremendously as he doesn't have to face me at the card tables. He also said that he stays in touch with Baudin, who also played on the Cobra football team in the Philippines. Baudin got a job with the Secret Service and is now guarding high-ranking diplomats," explained Cam.

"Oh, I received a letter from Michael. He said the wine yield has been fantastic. The sun shines brightly in Southern Italy and he misses us both. He said any time we come back, our ole' villa will be emptied and ready for us."

Abrianna arrived in Seattle. To Cameron it felt like the most expensive magazine in the world with a hot breeze on it's pages opened and the most beautiful model ever walked out of the pages and came to life. The hugs, the kisses, the sweet smells, the sexiest woman had arrived in Seattle. Her six-foot tall frame, long slender legs, braided ponytail, beautiful lips, perfect fingernails, and soft black skin were so seductive.

"Cameron, I missed you so much. I love you and never want to be separated. Just kiss me for a long, long time," she said.

They stood there kissing until a young lady asked, "Are you both movie stars? I know I've seen you both before."

They laughed and asked, "Would you like our autographs?"

Cameron took Abrianna in his car back to his apartment with the swimming pool. Even though it was a little cool outside, she put on a bathing suit and laid next to the pool. Cameron swore that the pool was only used by a few people at a time, but it now seemed that everyone in the apartment building was wearing their swimsuit and sitting by the pool. Many of them scoped out Abrianna's sexy body and Cameron's twelve-pack chiseled abs. Even though Abrianna and Cam were black, discrimination can't compete with sexy bodies. The couple nearly brought the pool to a boil. They both laughed at all the commotion.

They enjoyed their days together. Cameron showed her the many highlights of Tacoma and Seattle, from the awesome views at the Space Needle, to watching killer whales from the ferry, and viewing the tremendous height of Snoqualmie Falls.

Cam then took Abrianna to meet his mother and father. Interestingly, neither of his parents said whether or not they liked Abrianna.

He even took Abrianna to watch him work out with his karate students. She had seen him teach karate in Italy and was happy to see his passion for Karate continue.

Cameron knew something wasn't right in his relationship with Abrianna when they were in Queens, New York. He couldn't get past Gold Key No. 8, on real love. So if it wasn't real love, he knew it had to be a play date or lust date. Darn, he really liked Abrianna.

Later that night, Abrianna said, "I think I will stay with you, if that's okay. I will send for my clothes and I will get a job tomorrow as an administrative assistant or even a model if I can find the work. I will help you with the rent and I will take care of you until you finish college. I love you Cam. I want to be that special person in your life forever."

Cameron looked her in the eyes and said, "I think I want that too, but first I must finish college before I can commit to anything. Why don't you head back home and pack up all your things so you don't forget anything?"

"No Cam I do not want to leave."

"I know, but I have a tremendously difficult quarter with all my courses, plus football and Karate. So, it makes more sense for you to go back home and get organized."

"Are you sure Cam?" she asked.

"Yes, it'll only be a month or two."

"Okay." She kissed Cameron passionately. After extending her trip for two full weeks exploring Washington, Cam took Abrianna to the airport and gave her one last kiss, knowing he may never see her again.

That evening he called Abrianna to see if she had arrived home safely. A man answered the telephone and Cameron could tell that Abrianna was near the phone.

"Hello, is Abrianna there?" asked Cameron.

"Who is calling?" the man asked.

"Cameron."

The man said, "Abrianna has come back to me and she never wants to see you again." "I won turkey!"

Instantly, Cameron understood what had been troubling him. He sensed something wasn't right that night in Queens. He now knew it was another guy. She never mentioned him. Cameron had dodged a giant bullet by sticking to his 10 Keys to success. He was holding out for real love.

"No, you didn't win," said Cameron. "I'm giving her back to you. Have a great day." He spoke loudly in hopes that Abrianna would hear him. Cameron never called her again.

Karate was a significant source of pride and pleasure for Cameron. He loved the meditation, exercise, combat, and fellowship it provided. Thus, he elected to continue Karate classes for young minority youth in the central district. He charged only a few dollars so parents could afford to send their children to his classes. Word rapidly spread that he would be teaching Karate in a nearby church. Eighty-five kids, ages seven to eighteen, showed up for that first class. He taught the classes three times a week after school.

Cameron was really happy with the direction his life was taking. He had perhaps the fastest car in Seattle, a beautiful apartment with a heated swimming pool, he had just been admitted into the business school at one of the finest universities in the nation, and he was a second-degree black belt sensei teaching Karate to inner-city kids.

Back on campus he met with his college advisor. He seemed hell-bent on Cameron flunking out of the university. Cameron was assigned what seemed like the toughest, most challenging courses: finance, accounting, operational systems, marketing and business law. Cameron said to himself, bring it on baby, bring it on. He had now received straight A's in each and every one of his classes. He then asked his counselor, to approve an additional four credits of classes. "Why do you want to do that," asked the advisor. "I can't approve it."

"Well, I'm finding that I love college. I can't believe I'm saying that, but if I go on to grad school, my GI Bill will only pay for so many future quarters."

"Good for you, Cameron." The advisor signed off on an additional computer class.

Cameron now threw himself into his courses, burning the candle after football and Karate practice.

Football came naturally to Cameron with his years of experience from high school, Wilder College, and the air force, along with his rocket speed. He laughed to himself thinking back to one particular game in Italy where Big El had passed his bola bag to spectators and pumped his toilet plunger up and down to the beat of Sly and the Family Stone music. Beautiful cheerleaders, waiting to catch the big freighter to Corfu were there, waving their arms and dancing. It was there in Italy that Cameron touched the football five times and scored five touchdowns. All-American as a freshman and All-Air Force in the service, Cameron felt confident about landing a spot high on the team's depth chart.

"Cameron, the coach wants to see you," said the equipment manager. Cameron thought it was a little odd that the coach wanted to see him when he had never spent one second talking to the coach before.

"Price, our wide-receiver coach says that you only have one year of eligibility remaining so we will not be investing any further in your development. Thank you for turning out. Please give your equipment to the equipment manager."

Cameron did not expect to hear this from the coach. He was so surprised that the only thing he could say was, "Thank you for the opportunity to turn out, coach."

Walking out the coach's door, he knew he had been shoved out the door, but he did not know why. Cameron had received offers to play football for Texas University and the University of Tennessee when he was in the Air Force. Sometimes, things happen for a reason. He was about to find out.

Earlier in the season the NU football coach had received negative press about minorities on the football team and the coach kicked many of those players off the team. Cameron did not know why he was kicked off the team as he had never talked to the coach nor had he talked badly about the football program. There was a purge of nearly all the blacks from the football team.

Two hours later, Cameron was in his Business Government and Society class taught by the head of the college faculty.

"Are you a football player?" the professor inquired, no doubt looking at Cameron's build, especially his large neck. The professor had also come to know Cameron as one of his top academic students in his class.

"I was," said Cameron.

"Why aren't you on the team?" asked the professor.

Cameron then laid out his disappointment, telling the professor how the coach had dismissed him and how the coach lacked everything from player focus on offensive and defensive assignments, team spirit, and inspirational energy. In fact, not one player knew the name of the player next to him. How can you have a great team if you do not know anything about the player to your left or right? "Digest that," he told him. He went on to say the coach was surrounded by incompetent assistant coaches.

The professor stopped Cameron and said, "Would you mind writing me a summary paper on the condition of the football program from your vantage point?"

"Sure," said Cameron.

Then it happened. As Cameron began writing, he entered the zone that life had in store for him. He could laser-focus his arguments and win. "The pen is mightier than the sword." He had heard the saying many times, now it became his mantra. The mass appeal of well-reasoned honesty is an elixir to the mind. He was a natural.

Cam subsequently learned that his professor had been charged with the task of recommending his coach's future to the Board of Regents. The coach's win-loss football record did not help him, but when he read Cameron's letter, it explained why the record was so poor and on the decline. The coach was fired. All the assistant coaches were let go. Cameron's wide receivers coach left the university to take the head coaching job at Wilder College. He lasted one season and then Wilder eliminated the entire football program."

It was really hard for Cameron to say goodbye to football. When the time comes to hang up your cleats for good, it is like a part of you dies, never to get the call to go to war again because you are too old or injured. Warriors want to be warriors. They live for the battles. Cameron knew it was time for him to move on.

One day, Cameron went to visit his cousin, Brad, who worked at a men's clothing store. Upon entering the store, he saw a lady who had vibrant red hair and emerald eyes. Brad was standing next to her. Cameron said, with this trademark impish twinkling smile! "What's your name?"

She blushed and smiled back, "Kora."

"How long have you been working with my cousin?"

She looked at Brad, smiled and said "About a year."

Cameron had met many beautiful women but Kora was absolutely stunning. She really should have been a Hollywood movie star with her classic looks. Cameron knew immediately from breaking the code on love, Gold Key No. 8, that this was not the love that he was searching for but, "my oh my," was she extremely attractive.

Cousin Brad smiled and laughed out loud, as he had never seen Cameron so fixated on a woman. "Why don't we all get together this weekend?" said Brad. "I'll bring my wife."

Kora said it was fine with her. They had a picnic at a nearby lake. Kora and Cameron were a steamy item and she moved in with him about two weeks later.

Kora was really into Cam and told him she liked his happy personality, his keen mind, and his Karate and football build.

Cameron aced all his classes that quarter and then something surprising happened. Business students began asking him if they could study with him. Cameron said he would be pleased to help. After flunking out of college to now leading gifted business students in their class preparation, he was now achieving success that he never dreamed possible.

His advisor could only shake his head when Cameron showed him his grades. "And yes, I want you to sign off on an additional four credits this quarter." "Are you sure you don't want to take eight credits?" his advisor asked in a very serious voice.

"No, four is plenty."

Over the course of a year Kora and Cameron traveled the state on picnics, hunting, fishing, and parties with friends and relatives. Kora had a wonderful stepfather and mother who didn't object to their dating. Cameron sensed that they felt that the relationship would break off in due time and it would be smarter not to say anything until that day happened. Her parents lived in a beautiful home on the saltwater side of Seattle. Cameron made a mental note that some day, he would like a house on the water.

Kora's grandmother did object to their dating, but they rarely saw her.

Cameron continued teaching his Karate class. The young students enjoyed learning karate kicks, punches, and katas. Their smiles grew large as Cameron said, "good job!" Cameron thought to himself, if only he were rich, he would buy gi's or Karate uniforms for each student and teach Karate classes free and forever. After class one evening he talked to several of the parents about having a car wash to raise money to buy Karate uniforms. Cameron was surprised to learn that only a few of his students' parents owned a car. It was a major luxury that they could not afford. The parents agreed to find a gas station that would let them use water. They also promised to bring ten people to help wash cars. It was an overcast day, not conducive to having a car wash, so at the end of the day they only earned approximately about a fourth of the cost of the Karate uniforms.

Cameron talked to his dad about his monetary shortfall. His father was impressed that they tried to earn the money themselves. He agreed to sponsor the karate class if they sewed the logo of his business on the uniform. The karate gi's, belts, and supplies were ordered from Cameron's karate master in the Philippines.

Several months later, Cameron was happily surprised one evening when he opened up the door to his apartment. It was his sensei, Marshall. He had not seen Marshall since the Philippines.

Marshall told Cameron that he was traveling to California to live with one of his former karate students, Kennedy, who had a large Karate school. He planned to teach Karate and raise his family there. He also mentioned that because his father had served in the Navy during World War II and his family was granted permanent US citizenship. His plane had a layover in Seattle and he wanted to take the opportunity to deliver the Karate supplies and to visit with him.

Marshall asked if he could attend Cam's next class. "I would be so honored, if you could join us," Cameron replied. He invited Marshall to spend the night at his apartment.

The next day Cameron took Marshall on a brief tour around Tacoma and Seattle. They visited the Space Needle and Pike Place Market. They also visited two of his classes on campus, then Cameron took him to a very nice restaurant serving Hawaiian barbecue with rice and salad. "Tacoma and Seattle are so green and beautiful," said Marshall. "The rain here is really a mist, not like the downpours from the monsoons in the Philippines. The people here are very nice, the food here is very good, and the tourist attractions are wonderful. I can see why people from the Philippines enjoy Tacoma and Seattle."

Cameron's Karate students could not believe when they learned they were in the presence of a sixth-degree black belt. Marshall was wearing his white karate gi with his black belt and six red stripes on it. You could hear a pin drop when the students lined up in rows and bowed to sensei Price and sensei Marshall. It was a wonderful sight seeing fifty young students moving in unison through the challenging katas that sensei Price had taught them.

Cameron then bowed to his sensei and to his students and went through his powerful second-degree black belt katas. When he had completed the katas, sensei Marshall asked Price for permission to address the class.

"Yes, of course," said Cameron.

Marshall walked to the front of the class and bowed to Cameron and the students. He then went through his sixth-degree black belt kata that few people had ever seen. This was a master of the Go-jo-ryu style of Karate. He jumped, spun, adding a powerful roundhouse kick. With pulsating veins, his powerful fists rained blows on an invisible opponent. The loud noise grew louder and louder with each kick, punch, or snap of his gi. The students were mesmerized by the beautiful art form and the power behind the kicks and punches. Their mouths grew wider as their eyes focused on this incredible display of human power.

When he was done, his sensei said in a no-nonsense and matter-of-fact voice that he was very pleased to be able to join Cameron Price and all the students that evening. "I have something in my possession that belongs to sensei Price," he said. I have been closely following sensei Price's progress in Karate from the Philippines, Italy, and to Tacoma and Seattle. I have a black belt with four red stripes on it." "Cameron, effective this very moment, you are a fourth-degree black belt."

Cameron thanked his sensei. This was an unanticipated honor. He had again used Gold Key No. 1, study karate, to open up many closed doors, from rescuing friends, staying out of can't-win fights, to being a helping philanthropist advocating for youth development.

"Cameron, here are the Karate Gis and supplies for your students."

The students cheered with excitement!

Shortly thereafter, sensei Marshall joined sensei Kennedy in California to form one of the largest karate associations in the United States.

Cameron did not see much of Nelson even though they were at the same university. Their colleges were far apart on campus. He had heard that Nelson's wife, Irene, was pregnant, so he was pleased to hear the great news that they had a baby boy. Nelson purchased a very nice house and it appeared that family life and student life had been good to them. Then, one day, Irene received a phone call from an old high school boyfriend living in Texas. According to Nelson, the old boyfriend told Irene he still had feelings for her and wanted to see her.

After thoroughly discussing the issues, Nelson and Irene came to the conclusion that their love was so strong that no past boyfriend could tear them apart. Irene held strong that it was important to test their conclusion by going to Texas to visit the old boyfriend.

Irene was on the plane to Texas when Nelson told Cameron about all the recent activities.

Cameron said, "that was a very nice idea you came up with but you have a wife and child. Are you nuts? What have you been smoking? Very bad reasoning. Never put your family at risk."

A week later, upon Irene's return from Texas, she packed all of her belongings, left the house, and gave up custody of her son, and moved to Texas.

Nelson's heart was shattered.

On campus, Cameron was still surprised that so many students wanted to study with him. All of his classmates from accounting, operational systems, administrative organization, and marketing students knew that Cameron was the ace in the class. Just three weeks into his stock marketing class, the professor said "Cameron, your analysis of the management goals, mission, and in-depth research and analysis of the company's earnings, forecasted earnings, in addition to their research and development programs will lead you to be a successful stockbroker. I can tell already, Cameron, you are going to get an A in this class. I haven't come across anyone with your talent in a long time. You have the aptitude to be a very good stockbroker."

Cameron was flying high after receiving such praise and the news that he was getting an A in his marketing class, which would result in another 4.0 for the quarter.

Interestingly, Cameron had developed a bond with one of the guys in his marketing class who was also on track to get an A. His name was Kurt and he was witty and probably smarter than most everyone in the class. He also had an appetite for all-you-can-eat buffets and had a thirst for cold beer. Over a full plate of biscuits and gravy and a 12 egg omelet, Kurt asked Cameron, "What are you going to do after you graduate?"

"I'm not sure," said Cameron. "Maybe go to grad school for a master's degree, or I may see if there are any stockbroker jobs out there for me. What are you going to do Kurt?"

"I'm thinking about going to law school. I just submitted my application and if I get accepted, that is where I will be next year," Kurt responded.

"That's wonderful, Kurt. I hope you get in to law school next year. What kind of GPA did you have?"

"Three point eight," said Kurt. "How about you?"

"I have a four point but with some baggage from another university that I attended," replied Cam.

"With a GPA like that, have you ever thought about going to law school? You should apply," Kurt commented.

In less than a minute Kurt had motivated Cameron to see if he could get into law school. He knew his parents would be very proud of him if he were to go to law school, but ever since Wilder the thought of going to law school had been an unreachable dream.

He wondered, how much effort it could be to fill out applications to law schools. That night, he filled out five applications to different law schools around the country. He wanted to complete the application to Harvard, but they required a $250 application fee, which he could not afford. Nearly all the colleges wanted a written essay, so Cameron, knowing that all the law schools would focus on his early 0.5 GPA average, focused on how his life experiences in the military had motivated him to achieve success towards his perfect 4.0. at NU.

Cameron learned that he had to take the LSAT exam to see if and where he might qualify to go to law school. Financially, he learned that it was expensive to take the exam. He had no problem signing up for the exam that would take place in one week. Fearlessly, Cameron walked through the doors to the LSAT exam. His mind raced back to Biloxi, Mississippi when he took the difficult code-breaking exam. He sat down, grabbed the pencil and exam book. Later, he would tell his friends who were interested in gaining an understanding on what the LSAT exam was like, "It felt like I spent the entire day with my head in a meat grinder and when I came out of the exam, nothing in my brain seemed untapped."

He received an excellent LSAT score and learned that not only had he been accepted to a law school, he had been accepted by all the law schools to which he had applied. A lesson he learned here was what he would call "Law School, Target Five." If you want to go to law school, look at your GPA and LSAT score and apply to five law schools. First, apply to the top law school above your ranking (he called this your stretch law school), then apply to three law schools in your ranking, and then apply to the lowest ranking law school in the country. You may have to go to a law school on an island but that doesn't sound too bad.

His mom cried with joy on learning the news that Cameron had been accepted to five law schools. "Cameron," she said, "you have to promise me something. I know it will be a big decision where you will attend law school and if you want to go law school, but we have a Great-Uncle who is a very successful lawyer in Shaker Heights, Ohio. I will call him and see if you could spend a few weeks with him to help you decide."

Somehow, it's always hard to say no to a loving mother, so Cameron said "okay."

After receiving confirmation from his mother that it was okay to stay with Cameron's Great Uncle, he talked with Kora. He told her that he would be gone for two weeks or so to see if he really wanted to be a lawyer. He then asked her if she could survive without him?

She laughed and said that "she could."

Two weeks later Cameron was at the doorstep of his Great-Uncle's home near Cleveland, Ohio. Specifically, Great Uncle Terrence and Great Aunt Mary lived in the palatial suburb of Shaker Heights. Their seven story 12,000-foot, brick home came with two kitchens, a greenhouse filled with orchids and exotic plants, a wine cellar floor, a root cellar floor, a ballroom, dance, and orchestra floor where music was performed live, seven bedrooms, five bathrooms, gold bathroom fixtures as in real gold, hardwood floors throughout, Persian rugs everywhere, expensive paintings by world renowned painters, plus a swimming pool, a guest house, a gardener's and maid quarters, and a chauffeur's building on three acres of land. Terrence's chauffeur drove a large Mercedes and a Cadillac.

"Very nice to meet you, Great Uncle. My mother says so many very nice things about you and Great Aunt Mary. I understand you've been a lawyer for years. What's your specialty?"

"I'm a plaintiff's personal injury attorney. I sue on behalf of people who have been damaged by the negligence of others and collect huge sums of money. How about you Cameron?"

"I don't have a clue," Cam replied.

"Well, the first thing that you're going to do is to shave off that Fu Manchu mustache. It is not appropriate for a future attorney."

Cameron started to protest when his uncle Terrence said, "And that is final!"

Cameron complied but wasn't too happy.

Uncle Terrence and Aunt Mary were models for success. Aunt Mary and her staff cooked in both kitchens preparing delicious meals. The butler brought martinis, wine, and other beverages each evening.

Cameron learned that his Uncle and Aunt had traveled around the world visiting Europe, and Asia. Aunt Mary was most proud of her Persian rugs from Turkey and her full-length ermine fur coat from Russia. The expensive paintings on the walls were very enchanting. They had original paintings by Claude Monet and Edgar De Gas. Uncle Terrence and Aunt Mary were indeed socialites as they had many special guests and celebrities over for dinner and drinks. Mayors, senators, US representatives and one movie star client dined with Cameron.

Unbeknownst to Cameron, word spread quickly that Terrence and Mary had a handsome single nephew. Aunt Mary laughed out loud at how so many mothers wanted Cameron to meet their daughters. One night, Louisa, a daughter of one of Aunt Mary's friends showed up unannounced. The best way to describe what happened next was to say that this young lady with long dark brown hair and dark eyes, was anxious to start a relationship with Cam. She was all over him telling him the many wonderful things they could do together.

Cameron thought this young lady was sophisticated, mature, attracted to money and went after whatever she wanted. There were zero love sparks from him.

As Louisa was flirting with Cameron, Aunt Mary came into the living room and said, "Cameron, you have a long-distance phone call." "You can pick up the phone over there," as she pointing to the phone on the nearby table.

Cameron had no idea who was calling. It was Kora. It had been a while since they had last spoken and she missed him.

"Just tell me, how much you love me?" she asked.

Cameron looking at Louisa sitting right next to him. "I can't get into that right now. Let me call you back." Louisa said a few words, just loud enough to be heard by Kora.

'Cameron, who is with you there and what are you doing?"

"Nothing," said Cameron. "I have to go, but I will call you back."

Shortly after the phone call, Cameron politely said good night to Louisa. He said he wasn't interested in going to a party later with her.

He tried to call Kora back, but she did not answer any of his phone calls.

Cameron never thought for a moment that his Aunt and Uncle would try to set him up so he never told them about his girlfriend Kora, but as soon as Louisa left he told them.

Two weeks went by and the issue of which law school Cameron would attend came down to money. As he had rapidly completed undergraduate school, he still had two full years left of the GI Bill. Case Western in Cleveland Ohio or NU near Seattle, Washington were two Law Schools on the top of Cameron's list. His Uncle said he could stay with them through law school as long as he kept his chin and mouth cleanly shaven. All of his friends were in the greater Seattle-Tacoma area and Cameron felt it was frankly rather stuffy with the rich and famous in Shaker Heights. So, after deep thought, Cameron was headed back to Tacoma where he planned to attend law school.

Upon his return, he found that Kora had moved out. He eventually touched base with her. First, she said that when she heard that woman's voice on the phone she knew he had cheated on her. Cameron told her he hadn't, but she did not believe him. She showed up at his apartment years later with two babies, pleading with him to let everyone stay with him. She also wanted to get married. She told him the father of the babies was her boyfriend before Cameron.

While he liked Kora a lot, the children were not his and he had really moved on with his life. She had made choices along the way and she would have to live them. He said, "I'm Sorry."

Cameron wondered if he would ever find real love?

He briefly dated a very attractive Japanese girl named Robin. They were more friends than lovers. She had completed college and had a great job as a pharmacy representative encouraging doctors to recommend her company's medications to patients. One evening she came over to Cameron's apartment and spent the night. In the morning, the doorbell rang and Cameron answered the door. He could not believe it was Amy, his old Canadian girlfriend.

"Cameron, may I come in? I flew all the way from Toronto to see you."

It was awkward with Robin sitting at the nearby breakfast table in her embroidered peignor.

"What do you want Amy?" Cam asked, as she had now walked into the apartment.

"I want you back." She was looking at Cameron and trying to size up Robin. "I am so sorry about my father and the terrible things he said. I just want you to know that I will do anything to get you back. I love you, Cameron and I can't live without you."

"I am so sorry," said Cameron. "You should have called me before you went to the huge expense of flying here. It is over and I have moved on."

She started crying. Her crying turned into loud sobs. "Please take me back!"

Cameron turned to Robin and said, "Will you do me a favor?"

"I guess so," she said reluctantly.

"I want you to come with me as I am going to drive Amy back to the airport now."

"Okay," she said.

Inside Cameron's car the sound level went from being pin-drop quiet to screams with Amy pleading with Cameron to give her another chance.

As they neared the departure gates, Amy said, "Why in the world would you leave me for that slant-eyed China girl?"

"Amy, I am leaving you because you are exactly as racist as your father." Cameron opened the door and said "goodbye."

"Unbelievable," said Robin as they drove off. " It was so agonizing to hear her plead for you to come back."

"I had no idea she would say what she did," said Cam apologetically.

"No worries. I understand the situation."

Robin and Cameron remained good friends for years.

Summer break was nearly over when Cameron walked to the mailbox to see if his grades had arrived. They had. He opened up the envelope very slowly. Maybe because these grades represented his graduation grades from college. When the envelope was open, he squinted with one eye at the GPA at the bottom of the form. It read 4.0! Cameron did his happy dance blended with powerful karate kicks. He thought to himself that this had to be one of the greatest comeback stories against all odds. From a .5 GPA at Wilder battling painful discrimination, battling enemies abroad, and using or clinging to the Tuskegee airmen's endurance and fortitude by fighting racism. To the power of great friendship, and Karate had eventually moved Cameron to achieve his greatest dream of succeeding in college with a 4.0. Now he had been accepted to five prestigious law schools and he would be attending one of the leading universities in the nation, NU.

Back in Rhode Island, Big El said to Susan, "let's go out to dinner this weekend at Cedar Plank Restaurant. It's been ages since we've been there."

"My, that sounds lovely," said Susan. "You are so sweet Elston."

Happy clapped his hands together when he saw Big El and Susan walk in. "I've got your coats. Now tell me, do you want your favorites or do you want to see the menu?"

"Favorites," said big El with a smile. Big El was dressed up in his very best slacks and favorite purple shirt. Susan was so beautiful in her short sexy skirt and black silk blouse.

After the Jack Daniels came out and they each had a big sip. Big El took a knife from the table and clanged it on his glass of bourbon. Louder and louder he clanged until all the people in the restaurant were quiet and looking at him. "Ladies and gentlemen, I would like to propose a toast. This is my girlfriend Susan. She and I have been going together for nearly five years." Big El then got down on one knee and asked, "Susan, will you marry me?"

Susan's face was flushed and then turned bright red. She was so surprised and happy.

Big El held up the 2-carat diamond engagement ring that he had saved for months to buy. The stone was large. So was his love for her.

She looked into his soft puppy-dog blue eyes and said solemnly, "Yes, Elston, I will marry you."

The restaurant crowd cheered loudly and bought them rounds and rounds of drinks. The owner of the restaurant picked up the dinner tab again.

Several days later back at the condo, Susan asked, "When do you want to have our wedding?"

"I think we should get married after I graduate from the academy, so let's plan on a September wedding."

"How many bridesmaids do you want to have, Susan?"

"I'm thinking a maid of honor and four bridesmaids. Your eldest sister, my girlfriends from college, and your baby sister Mary Dane should be the flower girl," replied Susan. "How about you, Big El?"

"Cameron will be the best man. Then your brother, neighbor Peter, cousin-in-law Ted, and your old friend Christian Sharpen will be my groomsmen."

"Big El, can we get married in the stunning OceanCliff Castle in Newport, Rhode, Island.?"

"Of course, my future queen," he said.

"Do you like bagpipe players?"

Susan said with a laugh, "Those dresses and hairy legs are so sexy and I understand they wear nothing underneath."

"Okay," said Big El. "I'll take care of getting these Scottish bagpipe players. Doesn't your dad have a friend who owns a shiny classic 1927 black Rolls-Royce?"

"Yes, he does," said Susan.

"Can you see if we can use his car on the day of our wedding?"

"Yes, I will check," said Susan.

"I assume your mom, dad, and granny will take care of the food, flowers, drinks, and music?" Big El inquired.

"Yes, I'm sure they will. I'll talk to them about those arrangements."

"I will take care of the rehearsal party," said Big El.

They contacted each of their family members and close friends to tell them of their engagement and requested their participation in the September wedding.

"Hey Cam, Susan said yes when I asked her to marry me! I know it's a long ways for you to come, but will you be the best man in our wedding?"

"Congratulations! Of course," said Cameron. "You are my best friend, so of course I will be there. What day is the big event?"

"It will be September 15th. We will be partying all week."

"Cameron, I have another request."

"You name it, buddy," said Cam.

"You are the best dancer I know. After I introduce you as my best man, would you mind shaking it up on the dance floor for five minutes or so?"

Cameron said, "Only if you have a shot of Jack Daniels and I have a shot of Johnny Walker Red before I dance."

"Done," said Big El.

"So are you a Rhode Island state patrolman?" asked Cameron.

"Yes," said Big El.

"I can't wait to hear all about it." I will definitely be there. I wouldn't miss it for anything," said Cam.

Cameron didn't tell Big El that the wedding date was the first week of law school. Instead, he went to visit the dean of the law school to tell him he would be gone that first week.

The dean became very agitated. He said, "Listen! to miss one day or even one hour is a death sentence that most law students cannot overcome. Cameron, listen to me very closely. There are 10,000 people who applied for your seat in law school. For you not to show up the first week will completely jeopardize your standing in this institution. I'm not saying you will be kicked out of law school if you miss the first week, but in all my years at this school, I know of no one that has done it before. If I were you, I would not miss my first week of law school classes."

Big El was Cameron's best friend. He had saved Cameron's life. Nothing was going to keep him away from the wedding.

# Chapter 4

# Susan and Big El's Wedding

"You look great, Big El."

"Thanks, you look great too!"

"Congrats again on becoming a state trooper. How do you like it?"

"Well, I just got out of the academy but I love it already," said Big El.

"Look at this. It's my revolver they issued to me. It is a Smith Wesson Model 66 issued exclusively to the Rhode Island State Troopers. It is just as powerful as the .44 Magnum revolver in the Clint Eastwood movie. Besides the gun, they gave me my own car. Susan doesn't like the car at all as it really is a piece of crap. The car has seen better days. Everything breaks down all the time. Our Rhode Island state trooper's operating budget had been depleted, so they have very little money to spend on new vehicles for us. Susan calls my jalopy a wreck on wheels. I don't know how they can put us in vehicles like this considering the liability. Anyway, it's all my car, the flashing lights work, and I can fly down the highway going well over one hundred twenty miles an hour as I chase cars."

"Do you give out many tickets?" asked Cameron.

"Quite the contrary. Pretty much zero," said Big El. "While it's not the standard operating procedure, I have a thirty to forty mile-per-hour over the speed limit tolerance so any driver driving more than that I pull them over and I read them the riot act. I don't give them a ticket. I give them a warning. Second warning gets a ticket. When I was a cop with the city in Sterling, I never gave any tickets. The sergeant was so mad at me he wanted to fire me. However, my jokes, and accolades, routinely made me the hit of the police force so even though the city needed the revenue, it made it difficult for my sergeant to fire me. I know how hard it can be on families to pay these tickets with their hard-earned money and I believe there was a better approach to get people to follow the rules."

"You are a great man," said Cameron. "I wish all cops were like you."

Driving up Susan's parent's driveway, Cameron yelled out the window "Sano roo Nikki, sano roo!"

Nicki, the large husky, started barking and chasing the car.

Granny was the first to greet Cameron. She hugged him tightly and said, "I will fix you your special Schnapps drink, Cameron."

"Thank you, Granny," said Cameron with a big smile.

Susan came out next and hugged Cameron and thanked him for coming all the way from Tacoma for their wedding. She looked beautiful and radiantly happy, just four days from the wedding.

Larry Senior and Betty came out next and hugged Cameron. Larry said in his firm deep Finnish voice, "I understand you've got into law school so I know your arrow has been flying straight."

Helen said, "I made you some Kristiana Cringle."

Lastly, Larry Junior standing 6 foot 6 inches, came out with a beer in one hand and his girlfriend in the other. "Cameron, it's always special when you are here. Welcome to your other home, my brother!"

After a wonderful lunch, Big El said, "Here are the wedding plans." With a huge smile he added, "Today is our rest and party day. We are going to drink and party heavily into the evening. We will be going down to Snapps' Pond, have a wonderful sauna, and drink lots of beer. Tomorrow the rest of the wedding party will arrive and the guys will get fitted for their tuxes. We will see how much beer we can drink afterwards. The next day we're going to have a pre-wedding party at Lexington Hall. Cameron, would you mind helping me set up my stereo equipment from Italy at the hall?"

"Absolutely. I can't believe we're going to bring back the music like we did in Italy," said Cameron.

Cameron and Big El drank beer and laughed loudly. Being around his best friend was special. Laughter was everywhere. Cameron's mind raced back in time to when he was just a little boy and saw all of his dad's Tuskegee Airmen laughing as they reminisced about the hardships they faced in World War II. Great and honest friends were rare and special. He reminded Big El of the time they went into the bowling alley at Kessler AFB and bowled arguably the best games of their lives to win big bucks from two GI's who thought they were professional bowlers. They laughed so hard. Big El said, "remember Arthur and the senorita from Acuna who left his reading glasses twisted on his forehead." More laughter. "And what about beating the unbeaten Italian head quarter's football team when we brought in a bus load of tourist cheerleaders from Brindisi.

Rhode Island is an especially beautiful setting in September with its breathtaking scenery, historical landmarks, museums, opulent mansions, and spectacular coastal communities.

Many of Susan's and Big El's close friends and family members were at the rehearsal party. Cam hugged Susan's family. Big El's mother, father, two sisters, brother-in-law, aunts and uncles, nieces and nephews were eager to meet Cameron. Cameron hugged and shook their hands and told them how lucky he was to be Big El's best friend. Then the single bridesmaids arrived. First was a buxom blonde from Denmark with beautiful blue eyes. Then a Chinese American with the most exquisitely fine features, and then the red head from Sweden and the gorgeous brunette from Germany. Cameron silently said to himself, I am glad to be single today. So, Big El and Cameron said in unison and laughter, "let's get this party started." Food and drinks were abundant as servers brought delicious food and beverages to the guests.

It was here in a large ballroom that Big El picked up a microphone and addressed his friends and family. After introducing Susan, her parents and his parents, Big El said, "I would now like to introduce to you my best man, Cameron Price."

"Cameron and I traveled the world "free and wild." We learned that the heart of every great friendship is trust. Trust is why we are alive and why we are here today. Besides being an exceedingly smart man and going to law school in a few days, he's also a fourth degree-black belt. So be forewarned, don't mess with Cameron. I asked Cameron to dance at our party, not because he's such a great dancer, because I wanted all of you to see his spirit as it unfolds when he dances. Quite frankly I've never seen anything like it."

Cameron was the only person of color in the room, with the exception of the Chinese American bridesmaid. All eyes that had not been staring at him were now totally focused on him.

Cameron took the microphone and said with assured confidence, "Big El and I went into the service on the same day and we both got out of the service on the same day. We are best friends as we have been through heaven and hell together. We met many great military men along the way. If ever there was someone whom you knew what they were thinking without ever muttering a word it has been the two of us. We call ourselves "Camel," short for Cameron and Elston. We hated each other when we first met, but we soon learned that nobody could outwit us and nobody could beat us. We traveled the world, free and wild. Someday, we may be able to tell you what we did. For now, I would just like to say how happy I am to be here and to thank Big El for asking me to be his best man. I am so honored."

"Now, I would like to propose a toast to Big El and Susan." Beautiful crystal champagne glasses clinked throughout the ballroom. "Hear, hear" went the cheers!

Cameron gave the microphone back to Big El.

Big El took a shot of Jack Daniels and Cameron took a shot of Johnny Walker Red.

Music by the Dramatics, Get Up and Get Down, started playing through the loudspeakers. It was Big El and Cameron's favorite song in San Sabina, Italy to get a good party going.

With the first musical note, Cameron slid across the floor in his white lace shirt, now mostly unbuttoned exposing his muscular chest and his black bell bottom trousers that had a purple stripe running down each leg. His black patent leather shoes fit perfectly and looked very suave. The crowd smiled and then began to cheer as Cameron began to groove, grind and dance across the floor as the soulful music got funkier. Something happened that no one had ever seen before. Cameron thrust his powerful karate kicks with such intense velocity that yellow fire, then red fire propelled out of his pants legs. The crowd quieted as they had never seen anything like this ever before. The flames grew brighter and brighter. The crowd stood in disbelief. Approximately four to five minutes later, the song came to an end.

"I told you," said Big El with a big smile to the crowd. "Cam is super bad."

A huge round of applause swept over the crowd as a demonstration of their appreciation.

Big El walked over to Cam and gave him a hug. He whispered, "How in the hell did you do that?"

"I sewed metal sockets, attached sliding brackets and wires, so that when I kicked hard the batteries would slide and engage, resulting in colored lights in the base of my bellbottoms pants going off and on.

"I loved it Cameron!"

"You're welcome my buddy!"

The young ladies were nearly hypnotized with Cameron's performance. All of Susan's bridesmaids were gorgeous and single college graduates. Cameron liked every single one of them. Suddenly, a bell rung in Cameron's head. He had broken the code for a woman to know if she was in real love, or if she was about to go on a play date, lust date, or a fun date. Cameron would describe the broken code shortly.

Cameron had a wonderful evening at the rehearsal party.

"Susan, do you have a second?" asked Cameron.

"I just want you to know how happy I am to be here. I know this wedding is the happiest day in Big El's life. We traveled the world together for years and I can honestly say that I've never seen a man love a woman more than Big El loves you. On a good day, Big El looks like a Roman god and on a bad day he looks like a Roman god. I've seen many women fall for his locks of gold and his blue eyes. His love for you only grew stronger. What an honest and loving partner you have Susan."

Tears flooded down Susan's face. "Thank you, Cameron."

September 15th, the day of Big El and Susan's wedding had arrived. After eating a wonderful Finnish breakfast prepared by Granny and Betty, Big El and Cameron discussed the day's activities. Big El gave Cameron the two karat diamond ring plus the attached gold wedding band to hold until the wedding ceremonies. Big El also mentioned that he had secured the classic 1927 Rolls-Royce Phantom. It was a solid black beauty with expensive wood grain paneling and ultra-rich leather seats. "I promised the owner, who is letting us use it for free, that we might tie tin cans to the back of the Rolls but that Burma-Shave and soap would not be used on the car or windows."

"No problem, it will be taken care of," said Cam. What else can I do to help?"

"I'd like you to say a few words in a toast after the wedding."

"Done," said Cameron. "What else?"

"After you drop us off at the Hotel, would you mind driving the Rolls back to the owner?"

Cameron laughed, "what an honor it will be driving my own Rolls."

"We plan to stay at the Hotel downtown for two days then back to work."

"What? No honeymoon?"

"It was all I could afford after the ring," said Big El. "Anyway, we might not see each other for a while, so I just want to thank you so much for coming East and staying with us."

"That is what best friends do," said Cameron.

"Hey buddy."

"Yes," said Big El.

"Let's call Susan in here. I have something for you both."

"Susan and Big El, here is my wedding present to you both." Cameron gave Susan a small wrapped box. She opened it and inside was a certificate that said they were the owners of 1000 shares of Teleprompter stock. What is Teleprompter, they asked. Well,

I researched nearly every traded stock to see if I could find a sleeper that might present you with the most upside profit. Teleprompter is a company that believes that the future of television is cable TV with direct programming. I am convinced that if you hold these stocks long enough, you may be rich beyond your imagination."

"Wow, our first stocks. Thanks Cam!" (It should be noted that after several company buy-outs, Big El and Susan sold their shares in Teleprompter to pay for a washer and dryer and ultimately paid for a six week luxuriously honeymoon package through Europe).

The highlight of the wedding was Susan, of course, who looked so beautiful. Big El was a happy man. The church hummed with excitement. Larry Senior walked his daughter Susan down the aisle. The bridal party stood next to the preacher and the classic music, 'Here Comes the Bride' began. It was a perfect wedding with orchids and white roses. During the wedding ceremony, the preacher asked, "Does anyone have any objection to this wedding or forever hold your peace?"

Big El turned to the crowd and said sternly with his lip curled up and his hairy eyebrow raising up and down, "there better not be any objection because I brought my trusty gun." The crowd laughed and the preacher continued. Cameron handed the beautiful diamond ring to Big El. He placed it on Susan's finger.

"I now pronounce you Mr. and Mrs. Elston Royal. You may kiss the bride," said the preacher.

Susan's face was beet red and full of happiness with tears in both eyes. "My, that kiss was pretty good, we will have to have more of that later," she said with a smile.

Big El had just married the nicest, sweetest, and most beautiful woman in the world.

Big El and Susan, along with the wedding party, stood in a receiving line. Granny was the first to go through the receiving line and hugged Big El and Susan. When she got to Cameron she gave him a big hug and said, "thanks for being so much fun."

Later Susan turned to Cameron and said, "you know Cameron, it's a good thing I didn't have more bridesmaids. You might have died from exhaustion."

Cameron gave Susan a thank you smile with his head nodding up and down.

Cameron said to Big El, "When you kissed Susan, buddy, I swear I saw the love in both of your eyes."

After the ceremony, 250 guests gathered for a full dinner feast of prime rib, baked potatoes, broccoli, salad, huge Finnish rolls, along with champagne, Jack, Johnny, and other beverages.

There was a lot of kissing and hugging.

Cameron gave the toast where he said, "what the world needs now is more love like the love shared by Susan and Big El."

The wedding cake was seven tiers tall. After the last bite of cake, Cameron said his goodbyes to the lovely bridesmaids.

"Call me," they whispered.

As soon as Susan had taken her last bite, a Scottish drum beat loudly. "It is time," said one of the large Scottish men.

Big El and Susan walked outside of the church to the antique 1927 large black Rolls-Royce.

Cameron and the other groomsmen had tied approximately 12 feet of tin cans to the back of the Rolls-Royce. With Big El and Susan in the back seat, Cameron slowly drove the car past the wedding guests with the horn honking.

When they reached the hotel, Susan's burst out crying and said, "Cameron, thank you so much. I love you. We would like to visit you in Tacoma when the time is right for you, Cam."

They all hugged.

The beautiful wedding seemed like a fleeting dream as Cameron arrived back home to face his first day of law school.

## Chapter 5

# Cameron's View on
# How a Woman Knows if it is
# "Real Love"

M uch has been written on the subject of love. How does one find lasting love? This question has perplexed men and women for years. From Adam and Eve, to Romeo and Juliet, to clinicians, to seminars, to Doctors of Philosophy, to perfumes and wardrobes, men and women often spend a significant amount of money in order to attract a worthy partner. At best, when we talk marriage, only 50 percent of couples stay married. Or put another way, 50% of men and women with all the available background information known to them over the past thirty to forty years make incorrect choices when selecting a mate.

Cameron, understood how women should find a lasting relationship. Cameron was one of the highest-ranking code breakers during the Vietnam war. He cracked many important military codes and felt he had cracked the code for men to know when they met a woman if it was real love, or if it was a lust date, play date, or fun date. He described this profound knowledge in Gold Key No. 9 during his journey through Italy.

Suddenly, it came to Cameron even though he was a man, that he had just cracked the code for women to know if a relationship with a man was "real love."

Women, many of you know the words to the code already, but insist that it really does not exist.

By 2050, there will be approximately 4.5 billion women on this planet and there will be approximately 4.5 billion men cohabiting on the planet with them. While it would be a stretch to say that Cameron could identify with pin point accuracy the code of real love for each and every woman. Without any more fanfare, therefore, here is the general broken code book for women on real love:

Women have wants and must have priorities that can be filled with as few as one or two items to well over hundreds of needs. Finding a man with lots of money may be a desire, but they shouldn't exclude other desires. For simplicity sake (there is nothing simple about this discussion), let's assume that a lady has 10 desires, needs, or must haves in a guy. They can be physical attractiveness (eyes, ripped muscles, smile, hair, teeth, tattoos, skin color, height, etc.); personality (funny, smart, educated, charming, dominating, gentlemanly, or can be dominated); financially astute (wealthy, great job, great potential, good provider); well read; religious; have love of family (appreciates parents and siblings); loves children, loves animals: outstanding lover: no drugs and on and on until all the needs are identified.

A woman should take careful time to analyze what her wants and desires entail. A woman's failure to do so "will" jeopardize her future happiness and love. Many ladies select a guy because he is handsome or wealthy and skip a few of their key desires, later to find out the hard way that they missed out on real love.

Now, if a woman meets a person who fills "all" of her desires, she is close to real love, however there is more.

If a woman is amazingly in touch with her desired list of needs, and Mr. Right comes along, here is what is missing. In most instances, she does not really want love for a night or day, she wants it forever. True love has to not only fill each and every one of her desires, but her desires must be filled each and every day and night. This of course makes it even more complicated for that special guy, where her needs may change over time. A woman needs a man who can adapt to her changes.

When a woman finds Mr. Right, she should show him she loves him every day and night.

Many women agree with Cameron about the code. Cameron anticipates a billion-dollar industry on helping ladies identify all their bucket list needs. Some companies have already made progress on this.

# Chapter 6

# Cameron's Law School Years

T he first year of law school was difficult beyond belief. To help put it in perspective, if you are married or dating someone, by the time you finish law school fifty percent will be divorced or their relationships will have ended. Cameron quickly learned that he was so far behind in his studies. Law school gives each student, no matter how smart and brilliant they may be, more homework than is humanly possible to accomplish. For example, each night you may have to read 200 to 300 pages of intense case law and then write briefs on everything that you have read. Multiply that by four or five classes that you are taking. The amount of required reading, analysing of cases, and required briefings made it a nearly impossible task. The majority of the students formed study groups to help divide all the briefings and alleviate some of the pressures of the daily course work. Arriving a week late to classes, did not make it any easier on Cameron. He was now too late to join a study group.

Even Kurt, from his marketing class in undergraduate school, had his own study group. Kurt and Cameron would go on to become very close friends, but not that first quarter. It should be noted that Kurt was selected by his peers as the number one student on rules of evidence and would go on to accept a career position with a county prosecutor's office.

Cameron realized he could no longer teach karate lessons to his students and study his law school courses. Sadly, he contacted a nearby large karate dojo where the sensei agreed to accept Cameron's students at a very modest fee. Cameron depleted his savings by paying the fee for every student for one year.

He met a fellow black student named Ray, who had not joined a study group because he had to work as a bartender at night to help pay for law school. He had also arrived several days late to law school. Ray had a heart of gold, honest, was super witty, and made other law students laugh, when laughing was a forgotten concept. Study sessions with Ray helped immensely. Ray and Cameron were two of only six black law students.

NU Law School relied heavily on the Socratic Method of teaching, after the classical Greek philosopher Socrates. It was a form of inquiry and discussion between professors and students, based on asking and answering questions to stimulate critical thinking and to illuminate ideas. Professors at NU taught what Cameron would describe as a mean or no nonsense form of asking questions. Cameron would often tell 'would be' law school students to see the movie "Paper Chase" if they were serious about going to law school.

The first year of law school was painfully difficult. He learned fundamental concepts like:

- Caveat emptor
- Post hoc ergo propter hoc
- Do you know the holding in Hawkins v Magee or are you just sitting in that chair and wasting everyone's time?
- Legal Research writing on major cases such as Roe v Wade

A tiny sampling of "stare decisis" which is the doctrine of precedent courts cite when an issue has been previously brought to the court and a ruling already issued. Generally, courts adhere to a previous ruling, though this is not unanimously excepted. Cameron was, therefore, required to learn and understand case law at a rapid pace:

- Dred Scott v Sanford, 60 U.S. 383 (1857).
- Yick Wo v Hopkins, 118 U.S. 356 (1886).
- Plessy v Ferguson, 163 U.S. 537 (1896).

- Powell v Alabama, 287 U.S. 45 (1932).
- Missouri ex rel. Gaines v Canada, 305 U.S. 337 (1938).
- Shelley v Kraemer, 334 U.S. 1 (1948).
- Brown v Board of Education of Topeka, 347 U.S. 483 (1954).
- Miranda v Arizona, 384 U.S. 436 (1966).

Cameron buckled down that first quarter and studied harder and smarter than he had ever done before. He was able to salvage his first quarter of law school by receiving a 2.6 GPA, but the downside was that he had to drop two classes that he would eventually have to make up. This setback would make it hard to graduate with his class, but that was the last thing he was thinking of because each day he was in survival mode.

Nearing the midpoint of his second quarter, it was time to take his mid-term exams. He checked to see if he had sufficient quantities of "blue books" for the exams. Blue books were universally accepted blank pages covered by a blue cover to submit one's written answers to course questions. He was low on blue books so he drove his firebird to his neighborhood Pay-n-Save store. He walked into the store and over to the stationary supplies. He picked up a handful of blue books, stood up and turned to see where he needed to pay for the blue books. Then it happened. It was the most romantic moment that Cameron had yearned for so long. Between wishing and praying Cameron saw a checker who literally turned a glance into wedding bells. He knew instantly that heaven had at last brought him real love. And it just wasn't love at first sight. It wasn't a pretend wedding bell sound, it was a full orchestra of wedding bells exploding loudly in Cameron's mind. Cameron was 100% certain that this was the person he would marry. Now, how was he going to convince a stranger that she should marry him? He knew nothing about her. And she knew nothing of him.

As he walked through her line, he wondered what he would say to his future wife. Absolutely nothing came out of his mouth. Not a word. She said all the usual greetings an employee would say to a customer. "Hi, How are you, Have a nice day." He did notice her name, Michelle, on her store name badge. Cameron managed to give her a very nice smile.

Cameron went back to his apartment and gave deep thought on how he might convince this beautiful young lady with long auburn brown hair and beautiful soft brown eyes to go on a date with him. He estimated that she was approximately 5'7" maybe 5'8" tall. She was the most beautiful women he had ever seen in his life. Cameron had seen some beautiful women in his travels around the world, but Michelle was one thousand percent more beautiful than them all including Abrianna and Kora. Cameron was in love. This was it. It was real love. So this is what happened next.

Cameron wrote a note to Michelle that went like this: Hi, My name is Cameron and I am a first year law student at NU. I have a lot of potential. I would be absolutely so happy, if you would have a Coke or cup of coffee with me. Yours, Cameron Price with his phone number.

Cameron drove back to the store and walked through Michelle's line.

"Hi again," said Michelle, "did you forget something?"

"Yes, I forgot to give you this." He handed Michelle the note with a warm smile. She nervously accepted the note and gave Cameron a nice smile. Versions differ after passing years, but Cameron was certain the following happened next. As he walked back into his apartment, the phone was ringing off the hook. It was Michelle and she said she would be happy to go on a date with Cameron.

Cameron asked Michelle if she would like to attend a hockey game with him.

She said, "sure, it sounds fun."

Cameron called Michelle at her store after he had purchased the hockey tickets to let her know what time he would pick her up. When he called and asked for Michelle, a guy who answered the phone said, "who is this?" Cameron gave his name and the guy said, "I'm Michelle's boyfriend and she won't be calling you back." Cameron laughed and told him to say goodbye to her because his time with her was over! He reached Michelle at home three hours later and their date was on. It took Cameron about a week or two to purge the boyfriend.

Cameron picked up Michelle in his powerful Firebird 400. "My," she said, "this looks like one fast racing car by the roaring sound of the engine."

"It is one of the fastest cars in Seattle."

Michelle asked Cam, "can you show me what your car can do?"

Cameron smiled and said "watch." A millisecond later the front tires were off the ground. The thrust pushed Michelle tightly back into her passenger seat. The rear end metal bar streaked flames, and the missile of a car sped down the road.

Barely able to talk, Michelle said with a gasp, "nice ride Cameron!"

Their first date was so fun and flirtatious. Their conversation was sparked with increased interest in each other. They laughed and hugged. On the radio, Earth Wind and Fire played "Shining Star."

When you have that special spark of love for someone, it doesn't matter what you're watching or listening to. Just looking into those eyes was so exciting and the action-packed hockey game made it a memorable moment. Cameron couldn't tell you who played well in the hockey game or even who scored, but he could tell you how his love for Michelle increased as the game played on.

Cameron picked up the phone and called Big El. "I finally found her. The girl of my dreams, the one I have been searching for all around the world. Big El, she is so sweet and wonderful and beautiful and she loves me. I know she loves me. Michelle is her name. I love her. I heard wedding bells when I first looked at her."

Cam, I am so happy for you. Believe me, I know she has to be so very special for you to say you want to marry her. Susan and I can't wait to meet her."

Several days later, Michelle and Cameron went on their second date, skiing at Snoqualmie Mountain. Michelle was an excellent skier and so was Cameron. Again it wasn't their skiing technique that was the most memorable activity that day, it was the surge of love that was growing. On the ski lift to the top of the mountain, Cameron said he was too warm and he took off his turtleneck sweater leaving only a T-shirt. Michelle smiled as she looked at Cameron's large and powerful biceps and muscular chest. "Can I touch those muscles," she asked nervously? "How did they get so big?"

'I'm really into conditioning and I train every chance I can." He didn't tell her he was a 4th° black belt.

He smiled at Michelle. He took his left hand and placed it on her cheek and he placed his right hand behind her head. Looking into her inviting eyes, he slowly brought her lips to his lips. Cameron's brain exploded into colorful Roman candles that captured his emotions. There is no finer feeling than being in love, true love. Cameron could tell Michelle felt the same way.

They had a wonderful day on the sun filled slopes at Snoqualmie.

On the way back from skiing they stopped at a small restaurant for burgers and something to drink. After they finished their meal and were about to leave, two truckers came into the restaurant and sat down near Cameron and Michelle.

"What do we have here?" said one of the truckers. "A white woman with a nigger! I think we should kick his ass."

Cameron immediately stood up, smiled at the men, and walked Michelle back to his car.

"Darn, I forgot to pay. I will be right back," said Cameron.

"You be careful," said Michelle.

Cameron entered the restaurant and said, "boys, I heard you wanted to kick my ass. Here it is!"

The truckers jumped up and ran toward Cameron like bears charging their prey. Unlike karate movies where the fight scenes last five minutes or longer, it only took one swift karate punch to the temples of each man. In less than three seconds he had knocked them out cold. A little harder and Cameron sensed that he would have killed them. He paid the café owner, who had just returned from the back room and had not seen the fight. The owner was stunned to see two big men lying on his floor. Cameron told owner, "here is a tip for you and an additional five dollars over my bill to make two chocolate milkshakes. Give them to the boys on the ground when they wake up. Tell them, chocolate shakes are good for their health."

Back at the car, Michelle asked, "what happened?"

"Oh not much," he replied. "After talking for a few moments those gentlemen apologized."

Several days later, Cam introduced Michelle to his mother. Cameron's mother loved Michelle from the moment she saw her. "She is so sweet and so beautiful, Cam. I love her. I want to take you both out to dinner."

"That is not necessary Mom, I know money is still tight."

"This is a special occasion and I want to take you both out." Later, she took them to Canlis Restaurant in Seattle.

Canlis was one of the finest restaurants in Seattle and very expensive. It opened its doors in 1950 and has spectacular views of Lake Union. Its cuisine was well known.

The setting sun reflected sunbeams across lovely Michelle.

Michelle and Cam's mother had such a wonderful time getting to know each other.

"Are you from Seattle?" Cam's mother asked.

"No," Michelle replied. "I was born in Kansas City, Kansas. My father was studying for the ministry there. In fact, most of my dad's brothers are ministers. The very first thing I remember as a little girl were two ladies from my father's church who asked for my name when I was two or three year's old. I told them my name is Michelle Don't. I was often told don't do this or don't do that. So, I thought my name was Michelle Don't."

"Shortly after my dad graduated, we moved to a really tiny city in Eastern Washington. He led a small congregation there. I have two younger brothers and a sister. My dad wanted to help more people so he decided to leave the ministry and we moved to Tacoma, where he went to NU and received his Master's degree in social work. I don't remember our family struggling financially, but we all lived in student housing. My mom also attended the University and became a teacher. My sister and brothers and I were so young and happy we never thought we were poor. My father got a job with the federal government and my mom got a job in the public-school system. My parents worked hard and eventually bought a house. We got our first dog, Tammi. Life in Tacoma was fun. I babysat and earned money working at a retail store. My brother cut grass in the neighborhood.

We were so excited when my younger brother and I pooled our money, which was matched by our parents, to buy our first car. I was the only one who got to drive the car, as my younger brother was not yet sixteen years old."

"Cam says that you're thinking about going to college. What do you want to study?"

"Social work," said Michelle. "I guess I'm following in my dad's footsteps, as I would like to help people."

"Oh, Mrs. Price, Cam told me how you and Mr. Price met. I think you might find what I'm about to tell you rather interesting. My dad grew up on a dairy farm in Eastern Washington and his dad, my grandpa, bought an airplane. He loved to fly over the hills and valleys and streams. I remember him telling me as a very little girl, how much he loved to see dairy cows and horses from various heights in the air. Several years later, my dad met my mom in college and fell in love with her. Her parents owned a dairy farm in Idaho. My dad asked my grandpa to fly him over to see her. They landed on a highway near my grandparent's farm. There were not a lot of airplanes at that time and I was told that neighbors near and far came to see the plane. It certainly must've made a big impression on my mom as she decided to marry my dad a short time later."

Cameron's mother smiled at Cameron and winked.

Following dinner, Cameron reached for the check, but his mother beat him to it. "It's my treat," she said.

"I love her Cameron," his mom whispered, as Cameron tipped the car attendant.

Michelle had an awesome family. Her dad, mother, a sister and brothers were all very nice. Cameron was not certain if Michelle had told her parents that he was black before he joined them for Sunday dinner. Everyone greeted Cameron with smiles. Michelle's mom gave Cameron a tall glass of water as they asked him questions to try to get to know him better.

Cam talked about his background, his family, growing up in Tacoma, and serving in the military. He thoroughly enjoyed hearing about Michelle and her family. Michelle's eyes twinkled at him across the dinner table. He smiled back at her.

One thing that bothered Cameron was when he received a phone call from Minister Robinson asking him to come see him. Minister Robinson was Michelle's family pastor. The church had a huge congregation, one of the largest in Tacoma. While Michelle's parents seemed to be okay with Cameron dating their daughter, Cameron knew exactly what the pastor wanted to discuss. He had been down that road before with Katie Capriana from Bellevue years ago who was just a friend and the priest told Cameron, God does not want you to date Katie.

Cameron knocked on the pastor's door. The pastor, wearing his black clergy robe, said good morning. "Cameron, thank you for coming. Please come in."

Cameron walked into the pastor's office and sat at a table in the center of the room. "Cameron, I want to talk to you about Michelle. "God doesn't want..."

Cameron interrupted the pastor with such fierce passion as he had heard this hateful lecture before. "No, I do not want to talk to you about Michelle. I will tell you this: I love her and no amount of words from you will change my belief. Now, I'm certain you believe that you're a good pastor, but you're not. You need to pray to God every day that he will forgive you for what you've attempted to do today." Cameron walked out of that church.

Several days passed by, when Michelle's father called Cameron and said can we talk. Cameron knew that it wasn't going to be a pleasant conversation, but he agreed to meet. Cameron anticipated that Michelle's father would say that he wanted Michelle and Cameron to break up, but that is not what he asked. What he requested was as follows: "I know you love my daughter. She is young and we have made plans for her to go to college in Idaho. Her mother and I want her to have the opportunity to go to college. Cameron, if you really love Michelle, you will give her this opportunity. "

Cam felt that if he agreed, it might end his relationship with Michelle. He thought about the wedding bells he had heard when he first saw her. In his heart he knew that no amount of distance or time could break up their love. He did not want to stop seeing Michelle. Cameron was facing a very tough second year of law school and it would require significant attention. So, reluctantly Cameron agreed to go along with Michelle's father's request.

Late August arrived and Michelle and Cameron gave each other passionate kisses before Michelle went in her parent's car for the long drive to Idaho. "I love you," whispered Cameron, "and I promise to visit you in Idaho if I can."

Weeks passed and Cameron decided to sell his 1967 Firebird 400. He didn't sell the car because he couldn't afford filling it with gas, or having to put several new engines in it, or the potential speeding tickets that he might get. He sold it because he needed an economical car to drive to Idaho. He had never promised Michelle's father that he would not visit her in Idaho.

Law school had not started yet so Cam was able to drive to Idaho twice to see Michelle. She was so happy to see Cameron. They went on picnics, floated down the Boise River, and went to college parties. They had so much fun together. She even packed a lunch for him for the long drive back to Seattle.

The first classes of law school had now begun. No one loves law school. Of the approximately 180 first year law students, 110 came back for their second year. Keep in mind that those 180 students had very high GPA and LSAT scores.

Criminal law, Evidence, Uniform Commercial Code, Comparative Law were law courses Cameron took during his second year.

After law school started again, Cameron wanted more than anything to see Michelle but law school's challenging studies made it nearly impossible. Days turned into weeks and weeks turned in to months.

Michelle's first year of college was a big transition for her. She met and made many friends, but she did miss Cameron. She played soft ball and studied hard.

They did their best to communicate with each other. So, there was a letter here, a quick long distant phone call there. The difficulty of a long distant romance was showing.

Cameron loved and missed Michelle so much that he delved into his studies with all of his energy as a means of coping with his missed girlfriend. He would often study in the law library with his black friend Ray, one of the smartest guys he had ever met. Ray was broke and needed money so he worked while going to law school which translated in getting behind in studies and dropping a few courses.

When Cameron asked Ray, how he became a bartender, he said, one afternoon, he had read an entire book on mixology and later that night he found himself working as a bartender at one of the most exclusive and busiest bars in Seattle. Ray loved the tips and the lovely friendships, but instead of acing every test, which he was capable of achieving, he received B's.

While studying in his apartment, Cameron looked out at the beautiful May flowers when the doorbell rang. It was Michelle! She was home from college. Michelle kissed Cameron passionately. Michelle and Cameron were so happy to see each other. They certainly made up for all those long-missed kisses. It was pure love. Michelle was so beautiful thought Cameron.

"Cameron, I can't stand being apart. I wonder what we can do about it?"

"Why don't you transfer to NU so we can be together? said Cameron."

"I will talk to the University, and see if I can transfer," said Michelle.

Cameron's G.I. Bill was coming to an end, and his finances were heavily depleted. He was about to know the meaning of what broke felt like. School was such a struggle, he didn't know if he would ever graduate. Cameron needed to find another job in case he did not graduate from law school. He shared his concerns with Ray, who said he was also broke. After some discussion, they had heard that the FBI was hiring, so they went to the regional FBI headquarters to submit their application. It didn't take the recruiting agent very long after listening to Cameron and Ray to say, "Gentlemen, I will consider your application on one condition only. You each must graduate from law school and pass the bar." Dejected, they walked out the door saying, "If we were to graduate and pass the bar, there Would be a multitude of job opportunities."

Cameron had exhausted his four-year funding of his G.I. Bill on undergraduate and law school. He faced depleted funding for his final three quarters. He wrote to the VA about how proud he was to serve his country and how thankful he was for the significant education that the G.I. Bill had afforded him. "Funding for three quarters is all I need. I don't believe that the founders of the G.I. Bill program would have wanted a G.I., like me, who had has obtained a B. A. degree and almost obtained a law degree to be removed from his program due to funding. Your extension will help me earn my juris doctor degree where I will become a lawyer earning a large salary which will result in paying more taxes. I will no doubt pay an accelerated rate of higher taxes with the three quarters of funding that you would provide. I submit that I will no doubt pay for this extension in higher taxes within one to two years and I will also be paying much more in taxes as I advance in my legal career. It would also be a bad statistic for the V.A. to see a G.I. not graduate. Achieving greatness following military service, without this degree could doom me forever? Lastly, as a veteran, I fought daily serving our country overseas to help preserve freedom and our American way of life. Please take a moment and approve my request for an extension of my G.I. Bill. Thank you."

Cameron had never heard of a veteran receiving an extension on his GI Bill, but he was mistaken. Cameron's VA checks continued uninterrupted. With his persuasive letter and the resulting checks, Cameron knew he was on track to be a successful lawyer.

Michelle was accepted into NU shortly thereafter.

"Hi Michelle," said Cameron. "I have some really good news. The NU law school placement office helped me secure an internship position with the city's prosecutor's office for part of my second year of law school and over the summer."

In this position, Cameron would write memorandums to assist the attorneys in court. He also had an opportunity to talk with city attorneys about case law and their legal careers. Every story was different. Cameron knew that if he was fortunate enough to graduate, he would eventually need to make a difficult decision on the direction he would take on his legal career.

Cameron studied diligently during his second year of law school and his grades reflected the renewed effort improving to a 3.5 GPA.

Michelle also received a 3.5 GPA for her sophomore year at NU.

About a week later, Cameron received a call from Michelle's father. "Can we talk?"

"Certainly," said Cameron.

"Cameron, we haven't seen you in a while, you are welcome to come by anytime."

Cameron thanked him and said he would.

"Michelle says you did well in your second year of law school and are moving on to your third year. Congratulations Cameron. Would you be interested in working a three months' federal internship position starting in two weeks?"

"Yes sir."

"I'm going to have Michelle drop off an application that I would like you to fill it out. It's a position in my department. You won't be working directly for me but for the entire department. You would be drafting memorandums on federal projects." Cameron was shocked. He always sensed that Michelle's dad liked him, but for him to offer Cameron a job was amazing.

Cameron wondered why Michelle's father found and then offered him a job. Her father was a wonderful, loving man. It had been nine months since Michelle and Cameron were together with no hint of a break up. Maybe, just maybe her parents were taking a second, third or even a fourth look at Cameron.

Cameron followed up and quickly submitted the application and started work two weeks later.

The people in the office were wonderful. They all welcomed Cameron with huge smiles, so he knew that Michelle's father had told them that he was dating his daughter. Twelve people in the department would now take their turns trying to figure out if Cameron would be okay to possibly marry Michelle. Cameron wrote memorandums on meaningful subjects with the goal of advancing the public good. By the end of the third month, all thumbs were pointing up. Cameron really liked his co-workers, and had so much fun bantering on issues where every day seemed like a college discourse as opposed to work.

Cameron was really grateful for this internship position as it helped finance several months of his third year of law school.

Michelle and Cameron ate together and studied together every chance they could. They both did well in school.

Cameron's father gave him a call to see if he wanted fly down to Westport, Washington to go salmon fishing.

"Absolutely," said Cam.

On the morning of the flight, Cameron drove over to his father's house, then his father drove to Boeing Field. Dan Price, loved flying and maintained his own plane since getting out of the Air Force in World War II. He had owned several planes over the years, including one of his favorites, the piper cub know as the Henry Ford of aviation which was simple to operate. The plane took off after receiving proper clearance from the tower. Dan flew the piper cub on a straight path to Westport. The airport at Westport was fogged in so Dan flew the plane 10 miles out over the ocean where the fog had lifted. He then flew under the fog until they neared the Westport runway. They were now flying about two to four feet above the ocean. "Darn son, we are not going to make it." His father banked the plane hard to the left flying up through the clouds and back out over the ocean into the clouds. Seeing a break in the clouds, he decided to do a beach landing. "Son, if I can see, I can put this plane down on a tree." Dan managed to miss the driftwood on the beach and landed the plane perfectly.

They hitchhiked to their salmon charter boat.

Cameron told his father about Michelle. "She's wonderful, dad."

"I would like to meet her," said Cameron's father.

It was an excellent fishing day with Dan and Cameron both catching their limit of salmon.

They took a taxi back to the beach where they left the piper cub. There on the beach near the plane was a sheriff who no doubt wondered why the plane was on the beach and why it appeared abandoned. Dan sensed that the sheriff would find some way of giving him a ticket or confiscating his plane. The sheriff had walked way down to where the plane wheels had first hit the beach. "Let's go, son." They both rapidly walked to the plane and sat in their seats. Cameron had never remembered his dad starting an engine so quick and taking off. From up above, they saw the sheriff scratching his head.

A few weeks later, Cameron's father invited Cam and Michelle to go on a plane ride. His father wore a light blue jumpsuit and Michelle wore jeans and a colorful sweater, and Cameron wore jeans and an African long sleeve shirt. His father instantly approved of Michelle. "She is a very nice girl," he would say later.

Michelle had never flown in a small plane before and was a little nervous.

"Just remember, my dad is one of the greatest pilots that has ever flown an airplane, so you have nothing to worry about. He was an ace Tuskegee pilot in World War II."

Michelle smiled at Cameron and whispered, "Does that mean he will do loop de loops and fly upside down?" asked Michelle with a tense smile filled with nervousness.

They flew from Seattle to Shelton where they had lunch. It was a glorious day with the sun shining through the panoramic views from above.

Safely back in Seattle, Michelle said, "okay Cameron, your dad is a wonderful pilot."

Sitting near the kitchen table in Cameron's apartment, Cam stood grasping Michelle's hand and said "I have a cold, I have a sore throat, my eyes are burning, I think I am dying."

Well she said, "If you get some good rest, take an aspirin, and eat some chicken noodle soup, maybe you won't feel so bad in the morning.

"Michelle, is that any way to talk to your future husband?"

"What," asked Michelle.

Cameron showed Michelle an antique gold wedding ring with a very nice sparkling diamond.

Tears of joy flowed down Michelle's cheeks.

"Yes, Cameron, I will marry you!

One week later, Cameron met with Michelle's father for lunch. He told her father what a wonderful person he was and he thanked him for the job and allowing him to be a part of his family. "I would like to marry Michelle when I graduate from school, so I am asking for your blessing to marry your daughter."

"Yes Cameron you have our blessing and both Michelle's mom and I welcome you officially to our family."

Cameron would wait to tell Michelle how so many tears of joy flowed from both her father and his faces.

The next time Cameron talked to Big El he said, " I think I might graduate from law school in less than a year. If I do, I'd like you to be the best man in our wedding. I asked Michelle if she would marry me and she said yes."

"Yeah," said Big El. "We are going to have a big party for your wedding."

The third year of law school was about to begin. It should be noted that the attrition rate had reduced Cameron's class of 180 down to 92.

Cameron took Michelle to the law library one afternoon. He showed her the many law books that he was required to read and how he planned to attack them. Interestingly, Cameron discovered that no matter how much he tried to impress Michelle, nothing really impressed her. She loved Cameron. Certainly, she was impressed that her boyfriend was a third-year law student, but if he had been a third-year astronomer, teacher, or singer, she would've loved Cameron. Cameron indeed was a very lucky guy.

Michelle's parents invited Cameron to join them on a camping retreat near Kalaloch Lodge, Washington. They set up tents and cooked over open fires and had delicious stews and biscuits. They played sand golf where they utilized a small rock for a golf ball and hit it with a thin piece of driftwood. Holes were dug up at various distances a part. It was very competitive. Back at the open fires everyone enjoyed the s'mores. While it started out to be a very sunny day, by evening snow had begun to fall and melted channels of water flowed through the base of the tent soaking everyone. No one slept that night. Yet it was a time no one will ever forget, as it was so much fun.

Cameron certainly wanted to graduate with his class but he would have to make up for the credits he dropped in his first year to attend Big El's wedding. He looked at his credits going into his third and last quarter where he realized he would have to take 24 credits to graduate with his class. Considering that 15 credits was a full-time load for law students and 18 credits was considered a heavy load, 24 credits was insane, impossible, and no one had ever attempted to take so many credits in one quarter. That was the good news. The bad news was that looking at the academic brochure, it had a clause that said, anyone wishing to take more than 18 credits, may need to discuss it with the Dean of law school.

Cameron accepted the 24-credit challenge. But for the impossible class load demands on his time, he barely remembered one day to the next. It was all a blur with those long nights in NU law school's library.

A giant cobra leaped at Cameron trying to strike him in the face with its lethal fangs. The hood on the back of its neck spread wide with anger. It lifted its head high off the ground inches from Cameron's face and hissed. Huge beads of sweat rolled down Cameron's face. In an instant, Cameron was running down an alley in Angeles City in the Philippines where he was being chased by Hux who had butterfly knives in their fists. They lunged their knives at Cameron. The cobra stood in front of him preventing him from escaping. Just as the snake and the Hux were about to strike, Cameron woke up swinging his arms. He had been haunted by a variation of this nightmare since the Philippines. Cameron would come to understand it was a form of PTSD or post-traumatic stress disorder from his activities during the Vietnam War. The most common denominator that brought forth the reoccurring nightmares was stress.

Maybe Cameron should not have taken so many credits, but he wanted to graduate with his class, and he was under a significant amount of stress.

One class that Cameron vividly remembered was the Street Law Class that he taught at McNeil Island federal prison. He remembered riding on a boat from Steilacoom to the McNeil Island federal prison. When the prison gate shut and Cameron stood inside, he expected to hear absolute quiet, but it was not like that at all. He saw so many white and black men wearing the same blue green colored prison uniform. As Cameron looked closer at the men, he realized that he knew several black men from middle and high school. All were from broken homes, poor, and had given up on education. They had tried to survive by selling drugs but were caught and now were paying the price by serving time in prison. The men recognized Cameron and walked up to him. Cameron remembered them all, especially Terrence. Terrence stood about six feet five inches, dark skin, and was an all-star baseball player as a sophomore in high school. His powerful fastball had captured the eyes of many a pro scout and college coaches. He lost everything when he was caught selling drugs. Apparently, the quantity was so large, it earned him a special trip to this federal prison.

They asked Cameron what he was doing in the joint.

Cameron told them he was a third-year law student and would be teaching a street law class.

They said, "Yes! You are going to find a way for us to get out of here!"

The course was not designed to help prisoners get out of prison, rather it was designed to aid recently released prisoners to better cope with life and laws after prison.

Following the end of the course, Cameron wrote Terrence, asking him to share his letter with other black inmates. It was a code for release from prison that he hoped their attorney's might utilize on their behalf. Cameron promised to reveal this special code later.

Final grades for third year law students were posted on the bulletin board. Each student had been given a designated class number and the corresponding grades for that number were shown on the board. Cameron, had received a perfect 4.0. Yes that was 4.0 in all 24 credits. The vision of graduating on time with his class was in sight.

Not so fast, the Dean of law school wanted to see Cameron about his failure to obtain his approval on the extra credits that he took.

"Dean, I received a 4.0 on those extra credits. So, this is not an issue of whether or not I received passing grades, this is an issue of whether or not I needed your permission to take the extra classes. Dean, let's look at the academic brochure. The wording is ambiguous at best. It doesn't say I must or I will or I have to obtain your permission it says merely that I may wish to discuss it with you. Dean the word may is like saying I could or could not discuss the extra courses with you. I considered the verbiage and believed it was a financial term to pay the university for the extension of time for the extra classes."

The Dean did not like Cam's answer but he knew the wording was vague and given the 4.0 that Cameron received that quarter the law school might lose in court. So he said, I will grant you permission to graduate on time with your class, but I will put a star behind your name indicating that you graduated one quarter behind your class.

Cameron smiled at the Dean and said, "have a nice day."

Of the 180 first year law students that started together, only 80 graduated. Of the six black students only three graduated, including Cam's good friend Ray who graduated one quarter later.

Cameron and Michelle's entire family watched the graduation ceremony where Cameron walked down the parade ground wearing his black juris doctorate cap and gown (cappa clausa) with bell shaped sleeves along with purple bindings on the hood that designated law school graduate.

From a 0.5 GPA in his first year of college, to a 4.0 in his final quarter of law school, how did Cameron do it? Cameron was raised poor by a single mother and a father who did not pay child support. He benefited by growing up in a neighborhood that was great for raising children and where getting shot or beaten did not exist. While there was certainly a class difference, Cameron benefited from a very caring white family, the Nelsons, who helped raise Cameron like one of their sons. This upbringing helped put Cameron on a positive economic track through paid yard, house, and dog walking jobs. Nelson's parents communicated all the time with Cam that if he wanted to enhance his earning potential he needed to obtain a college education. The key to success, Cameron learned at a young age was to shatter this class barrier and the widening inequality it brings. Armed with this and the many lessons he learned from his war hero father, Cameron fought racism and he had won many major battles, but he knew racial tensions were still present in society.

Looking back at his educational experience since Wilder College, there were so many ways to look at racism. Cameron likened it to a huge maze with many false twists and turns with a hundred-pound weight around one's neck and a clock with a timer. Once time had elapsed, one can never escape the maze and thereby, become a statistic of a person with no education, no work skills, no job, no family, and a cell in prison. How does one navigate through life with all these obstacles? Self-actualization, excellent decisions, caring friends and associates help.

Over the years, many people have fought to the death opposing slavery and racism. Cameron was certain that many whites have wondered why the entire black race didn't form an alliance to harm all white people. Cameron first thought was that the U.S. was such a great country, its destruction was not going to happen. Second, Cameron read a study by the University of Washington, which indicated that all people are related from the first species of men and women in Africa. Cameron though this concept was amazing and wondered if the Ku Klux Klan would have wanted to hang blacks if they had known that they were hanging their relatives. Third, so many white slave owners interbred with slaves that blacks now have white blood lines. So, to harm blacks is like harming your family. Yet the color of one's skin continues to promote racism, and a minority of blacks will harm all races.

Let's end racism like many educated souls are trying to end terrible diseases around the world. We need to put a full court educational press in every corner of the world to end racism. We are all one big family. We all are related to each other. As Rodney King once said, "Can't we all get along?" We are all one family.

Along with this huge education campaign, we need to insure all people have the resources for food and shelter. We need to teach people how to invest in the stock market. While the time line for various stocks differ from year to year, Cameron believed that there are several industries that will expand well into the twenty-second century. We need to feed our family. Education was the key.

Cameron, having completed law school in three years and graduating with his class, would now have to pass the bar exam to become a lawyer.

# Chapter 7

# Cameron and Michelle's Wedding

B ig El, Cam's best man, and Susan flew in from Rhode Island
for the June wedding.

Michelle was so happy to meet Big El and Susan.

Susan said, "wow Cameron, you really found a beautiful lady."

They stayed up late into the night at Cameron's apartment talking about military days and life after the Air Force. Beautiful Susan had a heart of gold helping save people as a nurse in a large hospital. Big El had moved up the ranks and was now a sergeant. He looked great, no doubt from the physical conditioning he had received as a Rhode Island State Patrol.

Jack and Johnny poured smoothly as the laughter grew louder. "You once said to me Cam, I wouldn't miss your wedding for anything in the world," said Big El.

"I am so happy you came," said Cameron. "Days of happiness and joy are here. Let's get this party started."

"Michelle and I know this is your first trip to Washington State, so we have a lot of sightseeing events planned for you like the Farmer's Market, the Space Needle, Mount Rainier, Snoqualmie Falls, a ferry ride through the San Juan Islands and a King Salmon fishing trip to Westport."

"I really like Snoqualmie Falls," said Susan. "It is obviously not as big as Niagara Falls that we see on the east coast, but it is a lovely, enchanting, and a captivating scene of nature that speaks volumes on the lore of this natural site."

Past the high ocean bar at Westport, the fishing lines filled with silver and king Salmon flew around the boat. Michelle caught the first fish and would forever be know as a skilled fisher woman. Susan, Big El, then Cameron caught salmon and in record time everyone limited. As they were just about ready to head back to Seattle, Cameron asked Big El and Susan if they liked to eat crab.

"Heck yes," they said in unison. "We have blue crab on the east coast."

"I have never eaten a blue crab," said Cameron, "but I am going to take you to catch Dungeness crab. They are so sweet and delicious. How many crabs can you eat?"

"What do you mean?" asked Big El.

"If you tell me how many crabs you can eat, I will tell you how long it will probably take us to catch them."

"Okay, how about twenty," said Big El.

"It should take us about twenty minutes," said Cameron.

"No way," said Big El.

Twenty minutes later, they had caught twenty-five crabs using nets with the salmon heads for bait that they had just caught.

Back in Seattle Cameron's mother, along with his father and step-mother, joined Big El and Susan at Michelle's parent's house for a feast of fresh caught salmon and 25 Dungeness crabs on a glorious sunny day.

"What a wonderful party," said Susan.

The next day there was a multiracial wedding rehearsal dinner party filled with love, tears, to die for food, and partying to the music," Got to Give it Up" by Marvin Gaye. Cameron pointed to the wedding party and said, "let's dance."

The wedding party gathered on the center of the floor and began to dance with each other. Arguably, one of the best funk and party music of all times, the wedding party danced in perfect lockstep with each other to the soulful sound of Marvin Gaye. Friends and family snapped their fingers as the partiers grooved on the dance floor.

After the song was over, by popular request they played the song again. Cameron's father asked Michelle to dance. He pinned a $100 bill on her dress. Shortly thereafter more people asked Michelle to dance and pinned money on her dress. Cameron's sisters would later call this the money dance as 30 minutes later Michelle gave Cameron $1250 from the dances. This, plus Cameron's savings, helped to pay for a 17-day Honeymoon vacation in Hawaii.

Cameron's mother prepared a rehearsal dinner feast consisting of Cajun style New Orleans food from crayfish to jambalaya to Po boy sandwiches and red beans and rice. It was all absolutely delicious. All the guests smiled and licked their fingers and lips after tasting the fantastic food. Cameron's mom also knew that Cameron's favorite dessert was three-layer coconut cake and Michelle's favorite dessert was Greek baklava, so she made plenty of both desserts. Champagne, beer, and wine flowed freely.

The big day leading up to Michelle and Cameron's wedding was nearly at hand. Michelle's cousin from Idaho was the maid of honor. Michelle had six bridesmaids including two from her old college in Idaho. Kurt, Ray, Nelson, Cam's step brother, and cousin were groomsmen.

Laughter and happiness filled the large room in the Westin Hotel where Michelle had her bridal shower. Presents were opened containing sexy sleepwear, baby doll nightgowns so revealing the 24 ladies faces blushed red rose as they drank wine. "Cameron is the luckiest guy in the world," uttered Susan. "What a catch you are Michelle." The ladies drank to each toast. Michelle had a wonderful time with all of her friends and looked forward to her wedding.

Cameron and his groomsmen gathered at Nelson's home for the bachelor party to celebrate his last night of freedom. A large cold keg of beer, fine wines, and catered food got the party off to a great start even before evening's entertainment begun.

"We all really like Michelle so we are not going to hijack you and keep you from your wedding," said Big El.

Nelson said, "this party is missing something." The doorbell rang. In through the door walked not one but three sizzling hot ladies wearing a fireman's, policeman's, and a doctor's outfit. As the ladies started to rip off parts of their clothing, the doorbell rang again. It was Michelle and her friends. "Uh, Oh!" said Nelson to Big El.

"Go ahead boys, we just want to watch too," said Michelle!

Cameron sat in the center of the room and Michelle and her friends sat near the back of the room. After several awkward moments, the party continued.

The ladies danced and stripped and all the guys and gals cheered. Cameron wondered if he had started a brand-new style or trend for bachelor parties. Joint bachelor and bachelorette parties were a lot of fun.

"Today is the wedding day," said Cameron.

"What's that?" Cameron asked Big El.

"I have two flasks, one filled with Jack and the other filled with Johnny," said Big El. "It is not every day that the Camel team gets married so as your best man, I am coming prepared."

"Very nice," said Cameron.

"Here, buddy, is the ring. It may not be as stunning as the 2 carat highly shiny solitaire stone you gave Susan, but it is exactly what Michelle wanted and selected. It is an antique gold crafted ring with a 1/2 carat diamond."

"Not to worry, I won't lose it and it looks beautiful."

Cameron drove with Big El to the church for the wedding.

Nearly all of Michelle's uncles were ministers. Michelle and Cameron had asked her uncle Lloyd if he would perform the wedding ceremony several months earlier. Uncle Lloyd said he would be honored to do so. Now at the church, Uncle Lloyd who stood approximately six feet two inches with sandy blond hair and blue eyes, wore a white robe with the most exquisite needle work of holy spiritual scenes on it. The church had filled up with over 300 guests. Each row of pews had bouquets of white roses and lovely sprigs of baby breaths. Cameron admired the large colorful stained-glass windows that reflected beautiful warm colors into the church.

Michelle's neighbor started to sing. She played several wedding tunes on her guitar.

Big El motioned with his hand, pointing to the inside of his jacket, "Do you need a stabilizer Cam?

"I am fine. I just want to cherish these moments," Cam said as he looked out over the crowd of family and friends. Cam thought to himself that he never thought he would ever find true love and get married. This moment was a dream come true.

Cameron did not know it, but at the time, this was perhaps the largest interracial marriage in Tacoma. Interracial marriages were not an everyday occurrence in the Seattle Tacoma area. In fact, several states had recently legalized interracial marriages. **Loving v. Virginia** was a landmark civil rights case in 1967 where the U.S. Supreme Court invalidated laws prohibiting interracial marriage.

Looking at the guests, he noticed several of his great service buddies from the Philippines and Italy. They had made the long journey to support Cameron. That is what great friends do. They beamed big smiles towards Cameron.

Cameron laughed as he recalled the letter that he had received from his Mississippi service friend in yesterday's mail. "Cam, congrats on your upcoming wedding. Wish I could be there, but I can't. I just want you to know that if you or your kids ever need a job picking tobacco, I'll always have a job for you on my plantation here."

The church music began. The maid of honor and bridesmaids began to line up near the minister. Then Big El walked towards the minister followed by the groomsmen. Cameron walked and stood next to the minister and Big El. Lovely flower girls walked down the aisle tossing petals.

Then, the bridal march began, with the music that played in Cameron's mind when he first saw Michelle. He was so in love with Michelle. Michelle stood next to her father. She looked like the most beautiful woman in all the world. Her beautiful white satin gown with the long train was adorned with rich appliqués and brocades. Not only did she look stunningly beautiful, but the stained-glass windows sent warm rays of light on her. Cameron thought this had to be a sign from heaven. Michelle's eyes raced to Cameron's eyes. This was their special moment. They loved each other so much.

Michelle's father with tears in his eyes transferred Michelle's hand to Cameron,

The minister began the wedding ceremony.

Michelle and Cameron read love promises to each other. Michelle promised Cameron she would always love him but might not necessarily obey him 100%. Cameron laughed and said he would love her until the end of time, and then he would figure out a way to extend the end of time, as his love for her was forever.

The minister asked, if there is anyone who objected to this marriage to raise your objection now, or forever hold your peace. Big El with his pulsating hairy eyeball stared and glared at the guests. He would later say, who in the world, would make some public objection to a fourth-degree black belt.

Hearing no objections, the minister asked Cameron if he had a ring.

Big El handed Cameron the wedding ring. Cameron placed it on Michelle's finger and then she placed a gold band on Cameron's finger.

"I now pronounce you man and wife."

The church bells rang loudly as Michelle and Cameron kissed. "I love you," said Michelle. "I love you," said Cameron.

The receiving line was a precious time to briefly thank friends and family and listen to the many words of wisdom.

Michelle's mother and father had a wonderful reception for the many guests. When they cut the cake, Cameron took a piece and fed it to Michelle, but teased her by smearing a little bit of the cake over her beautiful lips. She laughed so heartily.

Later at the hotel where they would spend the night before traveling to Hawaii, Big El posed with Michelle in the hotel's honeymoon bed. Inside the covers were Big El and Michelle with a huge shocked expression over their faces as Cameron took their picture.

"Thank you Big El and Susan for being a part of our wedding," said Cameron.

"We love you," said Michelle.

Cameron laughed every time he looked at the photo.

Every day in Hawaii was exciting and romantic. The orchids had such a fragrant smell. Each island was a paradise. They strolled on the white sandy beaches, ate at fabulous restaurants, and drank many exotic drinks. The pineapple fields smelled sweet. Michelle told Cameron, the highlight for her was when he carried her over the threshold on their first night at the Kaanapali Hotel in Maui.

Cameron asked Michelle if she would go deep-sea fishing with him in Kona. Michelle had gotten a little sea-sick when she went fishing with Big El and Susan just a few days ago in Westport and was rather reluctant to say yes. But this was her husband's first request, so she said agreed to go.

Cameron found a charter boat that would take them out deep sea fishing in the morning.

The charter boat was very modern and it made them feel like they were about to be on an adventure of a life time, that is until they were introduced to another fisherman on the boat. Apparently, the other fisherman was a famous world class fisherman having caught every species of big fish except a marlin. He had booked the charter boat for a week and was now down to his last day. He had never even gotten one bite. The previous day the Skipper convinced him that if he opened up the boat to other fishermen, it might bring him good luck. He reluctantly agreed. Cameron and Michelle just happened to be the next people to call to schedule a fishing trip.

The rules were fairly simple when fishing for big marlin with a group. Each person takes 15 minute turns sitting in the big fishing chair, or the hot seat as it is called. Whoever is seated in the hot seat when a marlin strikes, even with ten seconds remaining, it is that person's fish. It was agreed that ladies, Michelle, would go first, and after flipping a coin, Cameron would go second.

Approximately 20 miles down the shoreline of the turquoise ocean, the Skipper put out fishing lures. Five minutes into Michelle's turn, the fishing reel buzzed. "Fish on" yelled the captain. Michelle was strapped into a harness and began to rock up and down as she reeled in the line.

"You look like a natural," said the captain.

"Oh my god, this fish is so heavy."

"Keep it up you're doing great," said Cameron. A short time later, Michelle had caught her first fish in Hawaii. It turned out to be a sixty five-pound ono fish, a prized high quality delicious game fish. Michelle did not get sea-sick and felt proud that she was able to bring in the fish all by herself.

The world class fisherman began to get excited as the fish appeared to be biting today.

Next up in captain's hot seat was Cameron. Five minutes with the lures in the water, a fish struck. It wasn't tugging like Michelle's ono fish tugged but it was a fish. Moments later, Cameron reeled in a ten-pound yellow fin tuna.

The world class fisherman could hardly contain himself as he was next up in the hot seat.

"Captain what are you doing with my fish,?" asked Cameron?

"I am sewing it to a large hook and I am going to use it for live bait," he said.

The captain tossed the live bait into the water.

Cameron sat in the hot seat with just one minute remaining on his turn. Then it happened, the marlin hit hard. Cameron's reel screamed louder than he had ever heard a reel scream before. The reel took line at such momentous speed that it started smoking. The captain threw water over the reel and said, "when I tell you to set the hook, arch your body from below your knees back over your head in one powerful motion. Are you ready Cameron?"

"Yes!"

"Set it now!"

Pow! Cameron had set the hook hard. The huge marlin jumped high into the air and raced away from the boat.

The captain followed the marlin as Cameron began the up and down pumping action to try to reel in the fish.

The sea was so colorful and the marlin was so beautiful that Cameron thought of the most fantastic marlin fishing movie he had ever seen. The 1958 film, The Old Man and the Sea, by Ernest Hemingway. Dreams often are made in minutes and Cameron was living a dream. Approximately 45 minutes later Cameron had caught a 245-pound marlin. Interestingly when marlins are fighting in the ocean they are vivid blue, but once they die they turn silver gray.

The less than patient world class fisherman turn was at hand. Nothing! Fifteen minutes had passed and not a bite.

Michelle was up next. Her luck continued as she proceeded to catch another sixty-five-pound ono fish.

The bite was now totally over and the world class fisherman was dejected.

Michelle and Cameron asked him if he would like to join them for dinner to share eating some of the fish. He agreed and had his family join them.

Eating the ono fish, prepared by a local restaurant, was one of the very best meals that they enjoyed on their honey moon.

With the tropical sun setting over the bay, Michelle and Cameron walked through the airport for their return flight home. Michelle stopped, put her arms around Cameron and said, "honey will you promise to bring me back to Hawaii?"

"I promise," said Cameron, as they kissed lovingly.

Michelle's parents' large living room was totally filled with wedding gifts. Michelle and Cameron were really overwhelmed by their families and friends' generosity. From complete china serving sets, silver ware, kitchen ware, sheets and towels to an ostrich egg, and even the solid gold Camel lighter from Big El and Susan. They were all heartfelt gifts.

## Chapter 8

# Cameron's Search for Employment

U ndergraduate and Juris Doctorate Degrees from NU, filled Cameron's resume as he searched for a job to support his wife. He placed applications everywhere, several on job tips from NU Placement Center. Cameron and Michelle lived in his apartment while he beat the streets looking for a job. He contacted many law firms. Jobs for beginning lawyers were not plentiful and it was proving to be a difficult search. Michelle fortunately found a job working at a pharmacy.

Over at his father's home, Dan understood his son's search for a job to support his wife and said, "son you could really help me out if you could manage a paint project for me. It is huge. I got a federal contract to paint a border station in Metaline Falls just north of Spokane, Washington. I will pay you $15 an hour plus any overtime that you work. I estimate that it will take everyone two months to paint the station."

"When do we start?" asked Cameron.

"Tomorrow. I will fly you over to the job site and you can join my crew."

"Michelle, my dad gave me a job painting a border station north of Spokane. He estimates that it will take us about two months to paint it, so I will work seven days a week for 8 to 16 hours a day. We need the money, but I want you to know that it's going to be so hard for me to be apart from you."

Okay, Cameron. Since my job will only pay about half of what you will be making, I guess I will have to be patient." After a passionate hug and kiss, Michelle dropped him off at his father's house.

Cameron always loved flying with his father. Each flight was so smooth as they soared over incredible rivers, valleys, and mountains. They observed the multitude of colors in the ever-changing topography.

"Cameron," said his father, "I am putting you in charge of the crew, so if you have any problems use your best judgment to resolve them and call me if you need me. The men are excellent painters so I primarily need you to keep track of everyone's hours. Just remember, when you are painting to always put a lot of paint on your brush. I made arrangements for all of you to stay at a very small motel. You each have a room that has a shower along with a stove and oven."

Dan's plane landed on a grass field in Metaline Falls. The landing was so smooth that hardly any dust rose into the air. Cameron carried his duffle bag full of clothes as they walked to the motel. There was one phone at the motel, but phone calls were long distance and very expensive so Cameron knew he would have little or no contact with Michelle. They walked to the border station to meet the officers in charge and later the crew. The Metaline Falls -- Nelway Border Crossing connects Metaline Falls with Nelway, British Columbia. The Border Crossing was open seven days per week from 8 am until 12 am. He learned from the officer that the Metaline border crossing was the number one border station used by drug traffickers to try to move drugs from one country to the next.

Cameron asked, "why?"

He was told that their operation had the fewest drug agents of all the border crossings in North America and it just became a numbers game as most people would get busted, but those that made it through without being arrested, made it lucrative enough to continue the cat and mouse game.

Cameron met the crew, and shook their paint covered hands. Four men were black and one was white. It was so obvious from their glowing smiles they admired Dan, the only black Tuskegee pilot they had ever met. Dan paid the men every week and was a fair employer.

Dan said goodbye to Cameron and the crew and walked in the direction of the airfield.

Cameron said to the men, "it feels like it is 80 degrees, perfect paint weather, so let's paint this border station!"

The painting began, white and green paint. Day in and day out they all painted. The men were excellent painters but shared little conversation.

Cameron rarely took a break from the painting, going eight hours at first, then ten hours, for several days, often up to sixteen hours straight. In his time away from painting, he discovered a small lake, which was really about the size of a large pond, filled with perch and crappie fish. Cam filled up a fishing line with fish that he had caught. He even discovered how to catch unlimited crappie. He took the tongue out of one crappie and used it for bait. It was like shooting ducks in a barrel. Cam would later cook the fish in his motel room. The fish were so plentiful that he never had to spend money on groceries. Cam ate fish for breakfast, lunch, and dinner. He wanted to save every dime he earned for Michelle.

Nearly a month had gone by when Cameron's father came to visit. "Great work son, it looks like your team has made good progress. I want you to come home with me for a couple of days. Michelle called me and said she misses you and wants to see you."

Cam spoke to his father about their hardworking crew and members of the family on the plane ride home.

Hours later and he was back in the arms of Michelle. It was a magical and romantical time. Time stood still as the two lovers cast a silhouette of one love. Cameron had to quickly return to his crew in Metaline Falls.

"Cameron, I got a new job. I start tomorrow as a temporary counselor at a local public school. I am really looking forward to working with kids and it should help with the rent."

"I am so happy for you," said Cameron with a kiss.

Walking from the airfield to the hotel in Metaline Falls, Dan and Cameron came up on a roadkill buck deer.

"Dad," said Cameron, "I am thinking about taking a lot of the meat for the crew."

"Deer meat is excellent if it hasn't been dead too long," said Dan. "This deer looks like it has been recently run over so I think you and the crew will be having a feast."

Cameron's father was right. The meat tasted absolutely delicious. The crew loved the roast. They laughed and told stories of what life in Eastern Washington might have been like 50 to 100 years ago living off the land hunting deer, elk, and eating berries for survival.

Cameron slept in the next morning as his belly was filled with the buck roast.

The painting continued with lots of overtime hours as well as excellent fishing for nearly two weeks, when Officer Grant walked up to Cameron and said, "your father is on the phone and wants to talk to you."

Cameron worried that something may have happened to Michelle or another family member because his father had never called him at the border station.

Cameron, nervously picked up the phone and said, "Hey Dad, what's up?"

"You got a call from a judge with the Pierce County Superior Court in Tacoma who is interested in hiring you to work for him as a Law Clerk and Bailiff. He wants to talk to you right away. Here is his phone number."

"Thanks dad," said Cameron. "I will let you know what happens."

Cameron definitely looked like a painter. His overalls were covered in white and green paint. He was relieved that the judge could not see his current appearance.

Cameron called the judge directly.

"Hi Cameron," said the judge, "I read your resume and I was very impressed. My current bailiff is leaving in two weeks. Can you start in two weeks?"

"Yes Sir, I would be absolutely honored to do so."

"Great. It is all set. I will see you in two weeks," said the judge who then gave Cameron instructions where to report for his first day.

Cameron could not believe his good fortune. Getting a law clerk/ bailiff position with a Superior Court judge was one of the very best starting positions to advance one's legal career, other than having a family member as owner of a large law firm.

Less than two weeks later, the border station was 100% painted and the crew and Cameron returned to Seattle.

Cameron thanked his father for allowing him to paint the station with his crew.

His father gave him his final pay check which included a nice bonus for completing the project on time.

Michelle hugged Cameron and said, "Cam, I love you and missed you so much. Let's try not to be apart again."

"I love you too and I totally agree. I have some great news for you. I think we may be able to buy our first house. Using my G.I. Bill , which requires no down payment, and with the income that you and I are earning plus the money my dad paid me, I think we have the income to search for a small house. We are ready to move out of my apartment and start building our future."

Tears formed in Michelle's eyes. "Do you think we can?"

"Yes. Lets go house hunting after work and on week-ends."

Pierce Superior Court Judge Boudin, was white, with graying hair, sparkling brown eyes, and had one of warmest smiles Cameron had ever seen. Cameron would soon learn that Judge Boudin was a very intellectually gifted judge who had a good heart. The judge was pleased to have Cameron in his court.

"Cameron," said the judge, "after you complete all the hiring forms with our administrative office, I would like you to contact the Bar Association and find out when you can sit for the Bar Exam. I would also like you to go down to the sheriff's office and complete all necessary paper work to become a deputy sheriff."

"Certainly," said Cameron. "Why do you want me to become a deputy sheriff?"

"I have seen just about every case imaginable and I expect to see some cases that I can't imagine, so I think it best if my bailiff had the power to arrest someone should they disrupt our court."

The sheriff's office was located on the first floor of the court room. Cam took the judge's letter requesting the sheriff's office to complete the necessary steps for him to become a sheriff. After being fingerprinted and photos taken, he stood before the captain of the sheriff's department who said, "when we get the results of your fingerprints, we will swear you in as a deputy sheriff. Welcome aboard."

Cameron learned that the next Bar Exam would be in four months.

Cameron called Big El to tell him, that he would be a deputy sheriff when his shiny new badge arrived.

Cameron and Michelle wanted to live the American Dream by purchasing their first house with the hope that it would lead to economic prosperity and social mobility for their family, all gained from rich and smart hard work. In was now 1977, and housing prices had started to soar. The average price for a starter home in Tacoma and Seattle was $20,000 to $30,000 and the concept of sellers receiving multiple offers had emerged. One month into the house hunting process, Michelle and Cameron found a small three-bedroom house with a white picket fence. The $35,000 asking price stretched their G.I. budget. In a matter of hours, the price escalated to $37,500, by increased bids. They submitted a security deposit in the form of an earnest money for $5,000. Shortly after, Michelle learned that the sellers were members of her church and she called them to say how much Cameron and she would love to buy their home. With ten offers on the table, the sellers selected Michelle and Cameron's offer.

They had a wonderful house warming party. Over twenty people came to the party where Cam and Michelle roasted a large pig on a large brick barbecue pit in the back yard. The succulent pig, potato salad, bake beans, salad, rolls, and a keg of beer were all big hits.

Back at the court house, Cameron was sworn in as a deputy sheriff and received his badge. Judge Boudin was pleased.

Inside the judge's court, Cameron observed divorce cases, criminal cases, negligence and damages, civil cases, but the three cases that Cameron will remember forever were as follows:

1.  The first case involved a dog on a leash, that broke its leash and attacked a young man who was about to paint the owners

house. The now one eared man sued the owner for pain and suffering. Washington State had a free bite law, meaning the dog's owner had to have received notice that the dog had bitten someone. Thereby the dog got one free bite. Thus, the jury returned a verdict of zero monetary damages for the young man.

2. The second case involved a young man with a rap sheet a yard long that came into the court accused of stealing a motorcycle. After the jury found him guilty, the judge said, "I told you last time, if I ever saw you again in my court I would throw the book at you. So, I am sentencing you to ten to twenty years in prison. He told him to sit at the back benches in the court. The judge told Cameron to call the Sheriff's Office and have them send a sheriff immediately to the court room to escort the defendant to jail."

Cameron immediately called the Sheriff's Office.

The young man walked towards Cameron and said, "this is terrible." I didn't expect the judge to send me to prison. This is horrible. I can't believe it. I need a cigarette."

Cameron told the defendant to have a seat and he could have a cigarette shortly.

"No," said the defendant, "this is horrible, I need a cigarette now." With that he jumped up and ran out of the court room and did not stop running.

The judge said, "get him Deputy!"

Cameron gave chase and in the center of the floor by all the elevators Cameron dove to tackle the defendant.

What was truly unique is that all the elevator doors completely filled with people opened at the same time and they saw Cameron flying through the air launching at the young man.

Cameron tackled him and managed to put him in a head lock.

Someone screamed, "he has a knife, he has a big knife, watch out!'

Cameron's head lock grip got tighter as he dragged the man back to the court room. It grew even tighter when he noticed the size of the large Jim Bowie knife. A sheriff deputy had arrived and Cameron told him that the defendant had a large knife. Cameron turned over the defendant to the sheriff and took several steps backwards. The defendant's lawyer put his arm around the sobbing defendant and said, "hey, not to worry, I will appeal this decision."

A large crowd from the elevators had formed around the defendant. Cameron ordered the sheriff to take the man to jail, now.

As the sheriff started to handcuff the man, he twisted and threw the sheriff into Cameron, and ran down the steps of the court house. Cameron gave chase. At the bottom of the last flight of stairs there was an exit door and Cameron attempted a diving tackle on the defendant. The man slammed the door shut smashing Cameron on the head. Later Cameron said, he felt like a cartoon character sliding down the exit door.

The defendant did escape for two weeks, until he was caught in Duluth, Minnesota. Eventually, he was brought back to Tacoma, and sentenced to an additional ten years on escape charges.

3.  The third memorable case involved an habitual drunk man who burned up another habitual drunk man killing him, as he stole his bottle of wine. This was a huge death penalty case. After a lengthy trial, the defendant was found guilty of murder but he was not found guilty of aggravated circumstances, so he was not sentenced to die. This was a major precedent setting case as it set the standard for all future death penalty cases in Washington State.

Cameron was taking a close look at how he might launch his legal career. Cameron felt so fortunate to observe many of the most brilliant lawyers in the state at his job.

It was now time to study for the Bar Exam. To become a practicing lawyer, one must pass the bar exam. Cameron had heard it was a very difficult exam where many law students had failed it multiple times. To aid his review, Cameron signed up for a month-long evening bar review course. After spending one hour at the bar review, Cameron said, "I don't like this review method. It is not for me." So Cameron walked out on the course. Somebody up there had to be watching out over Cameron as another black student who was also turned off by the review course just came out the door as well. In the entire course, there may have been only four blacks so the odds of seeing two black students of the same mind set, come out the door at the same time, was statistically astronomical. They looked at each other and agreed to study together. His name was Gerald, who by any standards was handsome and smart, yet he worried he might not pass the bar.

Together they studied seven days a week for ten hours a day after work. Late into the evening of the second week, Cameron broke the code on not only how to study for the bar, but how to answer each question. Cameron had stumbled on a formula for passing the Washington State Bar Exam. Here is the code: Watch the F-I-R-E.

Watch—First, bring a watch or clock to the bar exam. When the examiner says, "you may begin." write down the time and how much time you have to answer each question. Look at your clock every 30 minutes. One must pace oneself through each and every question. This is absolutely critical as most people fail to pass the bar exam because they run out of time and get zero credit for the questions that they do not answer. Write your answers quickly.

Now, answer each bar exam question as follows:

F- Write down what are the key FACTS of the bar exam question.
I- Write down what are the key ISSUES raised by the facts.
R- Write down what is the RULE of law that applies to the issues.
E- For extra credit, write down what are the EXCEPTIONS to the rule of law.

To get to the point of immediate recall of facts, issues, rules, and exceptions to the rule of law means tremendous devotion and memory of all areas of law. Cameron's hint to help you know when you are close to being ready to take the bar exam is when you obtain a temporal or spiritual feeling occurring once in a life time.

Gerald and Cameron took great pains to study diligently on every legal subject. Now it was time to sit for the three-day bar exam.

Gerald and Cameron did not know how the exam went for them, but they both thought they had a good feeling. Several weeks later they learned that they both had passed the Bar Exam. Gerald would go on to be a top-notch lawyer for one of the larger law firms in the state.

The judge held a big party after hours in the court room with balloons, cake, and coffee celebrating Cameron's passing the bar. He said, "I am so happy for you. In six months, it will be time for you to move on, so be thinking about your next career step."

About a week later, the judge asked Cameron to visit him in his Chamber.

Inside the judge's chambers, Judge Boudin said, "Cameron, I wonder if you can help me with something. I have heard from so many young people that are searching to find their birth parents and parents that are searching to find their child that they gave up for adoption. Cameron, would you mind searching the laws in all 50 states to see if there might be a way for us to put these people in contact with each other?

Cameron, immediately thought of Morgan, his son that Sharon had adopted out. In an instant Cameron knew that if he was successful, it would lay the foundation for his son to find him if he wanted.

When Cameron was not engaged in his court room duties, he was in the law library researching laws on adoption in every state. About two months into his research, he found it. It was just a tiny passage in Minnesota formulating possible first steps to allow a child to find his or her biological parents. Cameron showed the judge what he had found. Shortly after, the judge designed a local court rule that was approved unanimously by the superior court judges to allow children through a confidential intermediary to locate the birth parent. If the birth parent wished to meet their child they were put in contact with each other. If the birth parent said no, a period of two months must pass and the confidential intermediary must re-contact the birth parent to see if they would like to meet their child. If they say no a second time the records would be forever sealed. Similar steps were outlined for a parent to search and meet their child after turning twenty-one. This court rule would become to be known as the Tacoma Adoptive Rights Movement. Eventually it would spread all across the country. The warm-hearted judge indeed had found a way to impact so many people by helping birth parents to locate his or her child and a child to find his or her birth parent(s).

The judge thanked Cameron for his legal research.

Now it was time to focus on his next career step.

Cameron had received an offer to work in the prosecutor's office which would be an excellent step to serve the public and a major step if one wanted to pursue a career in politics. Then there was "the" law firm. Cameron had received an offer from one of the largest law firms in town. He could come on board as an associate working on a variety of legal fields for five years. After five years, he would have to make partner and would have a defined specialty. The salary for this position was high. Then there was an offer from a Fortune 500 corporation that Cameron had never heard of before.

Two days before his interview, he went to visit the corporation and looked at the executives walking to and from the elevators. The first thing he noticed was they all wore navy blue suits with white shirts and no handkerchiefs in their lapel pockets as Cameron liked to wear. His focus was on Gold Key No. 4 that provided that one must dress for success and interview looking exactly like the person doing the interview.

During Cameron's interview, the corporative executives said, "Young man, based on the stellar feedback we have received from Judge Boudin, if you are willing to roll up your sleeves and travel around the world for two years and learn every facet of our corporation from the ground up, we will make you a junior executive of our corporation with a sling shot opportunity to rise to the top of our corporation. And yes, we will pay you double what big law firms are paying."

Michelle and Cameron agreed, "the gates of opportunity had opened and Cameron knew his next steps."

Cameron agreed to accept the position with the corporation with one caveat. He asked to delay his start date as he had planned to take Michelle on a little trip. Actually, it would be a six-week vacation with Big El and Susan traveling from the Netherlands, down to Italy, and eventually Greece, and Turkey.

The company approved Cameron's request and within days after saying goodbye to his favorite judge, Cameron and Michelle were with Big El and Susan in the Netherlands.

# Chapter 9
# Big El and Cameron's Reunion

Eel sandwiches, veal, escargot, roasted chicken, fine aged cheese, and pale lager were some of the tasty treats sampled by Susan, Michelle, Big El, and Cameron. Johnny Walker and Jack Daniels flowed smoothly throughout Europe. They were on the vacation of a life time. The weather was perfect, and never rained, which was a nice break from the weather at home. Susan and Michelle got along well and were becoming great friends. It was one big party after another, only the cities changed. From Amsterdam to Rotterdam, they took boat rides along the water canals, listened to music near the famous red-light bars, and slept in a small room advertised as a room where Bach had slept. The smell of legalized marijuana was especially prevalent around the bars. It was a festive time with young and old playing with six-feet chess pieces in the downtown square bazaar. Museums, massive marinas, and historical sites were in most cities just around the next corner.

Susan and Michelle were attractive Americans, turning the heads of locals and tourists. As the slight wind rustled the leaves in the park, their short shorts were like a strong head wind, turning the men around to gather another glance at the lovely ladies.

Big El and Cameron were so in love with their wives. "Without a care in the world, I wish these days would last forever," said Big El. "Being in love is what life is all about."

There were so many highlights on the trip. Big El laughing and diving for coins with all of his clothes on in Trevi Fountain in Rome. They walked inside the largest amphitheater ever built, the Coliseum in Rome, where they could imagine gladiators entertaining audiences of the Roman Empire. Cameron and Big El kissed their spouses inside the Blue Grotto, rode donkeys up the rugged terrain of Santorini, and bargained with vendors for silk rugs in Turkey and Greece. They bought magnificent jewelry, fine clothes, and leather shoes in Florence. Their spouses peered at Michelangelo's David at the Accademia Gallery. They laughed at Cameron as he negotiated with a Turkish vendor who was selling a table cloth. The vendor wanted $100, and tried to speak in every dialect known to man to tell Cameron how much he wanted. Cameron responded in gibberish frustrating the vendor. English, Spanish, Portuguese, Arabic, and Chinese languages were tried by the vendor again. Cameron talked gibberish so loud and threw the table cloth on the table of fabric. He handed the vendor $20 who accepted the money gladly to get Cameron to leave his shop. They rode in a decorated taxi on the Island of Rhodes in Greece. The taxi driver claimed that he had given a ride in his taxi to President Kennedy and his wife Jacqueline in the early 1960s. He even pointed to a picture of them standing beside his taxi.

"I am going to take you to Mrs. Kennedy's favorite shop if you would like," he said. Michelle and Susan left the coastal shop each with an adorable black laced head scarf.

Michelle was so lucky as she would often find a dollar here a dollar there, and even $30 on the ground. She was like her own cash machine with money found nearly every other day. She always put the money towards dinner or entertainment for everyone. She said, if she found any identification she would turn it over to authorities.

The girls were so cute in their sexy short shorts. Big El and Cameron laughed as the girls drove the Italian men crazy. They wanted to pinch their butts but they did not dare with Big El and Cameron nearby.

The big highlight, of course, was returning to Big El's and Cameron's Italian villa in San Sabina. Michael, their dear friend, and landlord, had removed the servicemen staying in the villa for a week to allow Big El and Cameron, and their spouses to stay in their old beautiful villa. With family and old Italian friends, Marina, Michael's spouse, prepared a 20-course meal that started at 4 pm and continued well beyond midnight. Miguel brought out his aged, foot stomped grape wine along with bottles and bottles of delicious and tasty Italian liquors. Before every entre Michael made a toast. He hired an outstanding band that serenaded everyone with festive Italian music.

"Life together with you both is exciting and enchanting. I am so happy to be together again," said Michael. They raised their glasses and said in unison, "Ogli Ahgla," their magic words saying that life is better than okay. They drank the wine and laughed loudly.

Sadly, they said their good-byes to Michael, Marina, and their Italian friends.

On the train ride to Naples, Cameron asked Big El, "were you a little nervous about the mob learning that you were back in Italy?" Cameron remembered when Big El, years ago sold bottles of liquor and cigarettes to the Mafia with a promise to return with more merchandise. Big El told Cameron of the hand guns and shot guns that were aimed at him until the consulary smiled and said he knew he would return and not disappoint him. Years passed by and Big El never returned with the promised liquor or cigarettes.

"Yes, especially, last night when Michael's guards were drunker than us. I definitely kept an eye on cars entering our streets. I was prepared to pay a penalty, however, but not with our lives."

"Big El, you are the one of the bravest men I know, definitely one of the craziest."

They arrived safely in Naples but were lost finding their way to the airport. Big El said, "I will go find a taxi if you stay and protect our wives." Big El was gone less than thirty seconds when a gang of Naples thugs circled Michelle, Susan, Cameron, and their luggage. Cameron told the girls to circle the luggage, pointing to a nearby corner of the train station and he would circle them. There were five men getting closer and closer to Cameron. Cameron was not going to let them have the luggage or the girls. Closing in, Cameron shouted in Italian "vai fuori di qui!," get out of here! Cameron began to kick his legs with such power that it sounded like "Whack, Whack, Whack." The men were shocked at Cameron's kicking skills. They stayed just outside Cameron's kicking zone. Cameron stared fiercely into the eyes of the man closest to him and then screamed, "No!" The thug lurched forward to attack Cameron. In less time than it takes to blink an eye, the thug was rolling on the ground in excruciating pain. Cameron had hit him hard in the throat but did not kill him. The other thugs tried to steal some of the luggage but the brave girls would not let them and when Cameron came to their aid, the thugs, having seen what Cameron did to their leader, took off running. Eventually, the guy on the ground crawled and then ran away.

"Cam," said Michelle, "nice moves honey."

Big El returned with a taxi as Susan hugged him and told him what had happened. "That is why I left you with Cameron," he said smiling and winking at Cameron. Looking back from the taxi window at the corner where all the action had occurred, Big El and Cameron noticed that the men had returned to the site with more men.

At the airport, they were told there were no more seats on the jet. They all needed to start work and if they did not catch this plane, they would be late for work. Eventually, Big El and Cameron met with the President of Alitalia Airlines, who after listening to their pleas, issued boarding passes to them. Let's just say that Big El had a Cop's badge and Cameron had a Sheriff's badge. They rode first class, thanks to the President, which was the only way to fly!

# Chapter 10

# Cameron in Corporate America

After two years in the field, working at company sites around the world, Cameron sat in the Boardroom with four other candidates who were vying for junior executive positions within the corporation. If selected, one's future salary would be bench-marked from the bidding that was about to take place. Each candidate would stand and the bidding would begin on the salary a department or division would pay to hire the individual.

Cameron had met the other candidates:

1.  Drew was extremely bright, handsome, and articulate man. He stood six feet two inches, had brownish blonde hair, and brown eyes. He had a masters degree from an impressive Ivy League school. Not only would he go on to excel in business, corporate business, he was well connected to the Chairman's family.
2.  Sally was so gifted she spoke five languages and also had a masters degree. She was married to a stay at home husband, which was rare in the 70s. She said she enjoyed being the bread winner and taking care of him.
3.  Bill had a master's degree and excelled in a new field called operation systems, or the early study of computers. He was a walking genius.
4.  Paul also had a master's degree in finance. Cameron and Paul would spend many hours talking about stocks and bonds.

It should be noted that Cameron was the only Attorney and the only black man to have ever been invited to be tested for a junior executive slot.

The bidding started. It was intense. Management thought this was one of the best crop of candidates in years so they increased their bids in hopes of selecting an individual to join their team. It was fast and furious. All five candidates were selected for a junior executive position within the corporation. What was amazing is that Cameron and Drew broke the bank on bids received on their starting salary from the corresponding divisions that they soon would be working, They each received double the starting salaries as the other candidates and all previous candidates. Cameron heard later that when the Chairman learned of the high salaries, he canceled the program. Five years later the program resumed with a standard pay scale range.

Cameron and Drew told each other how much they were offered. Drew would be starting his career in the product assembly division as a section manager. Their bond would last throughout their careers. Cameron thought Drew was a great friend. He was honest, sharp, full of integrity and introduced Cameron to fine wine with oysters and clams.

The Law Department had outbid the Finance Department for Cameron's Services. Nearly a year and a half into the junior executive program, Cameron worked for the General Counsel who asked him to meet with the Director of Public Affairs. The Director said, "Cameron we have a very difficult situation brewing in Congress. They want to expand the safety laws, that if approved would stop all of product production for six months to a year. We want you to research the entire issue and see if there is a way we can stop or kill this proposed legislation."

"Absolutely," said Cameron. "What is your time table?"

"Three weeks tops," said the Director.

NU Law School's legal research and writing program more than prepared Cameron for this moment. At first, he thought the assignment seemed daunting if not impossible, but it was relatively easy once he discovered the standard on what congressional legislation could and could not do. Specifically, legislation that sets standards was permissible, while legislation that mandates performance standards was not permissible. Congress proposed action was, therefore, statutorily unenforceable.

Two weeks later, Cameron met with the General Counsel where he delivered his fifty-page memorandum crushing Congress's attempt to mandate performance standards on the company. Cameron's memo was not anti-safety but a report on how Congress was not following its own rules.

Two months later, working in the field, Cameron received a call from the General Counsel. "I want you to know that the Director of Public Affairs used 100% of your memorandum in Congress. I am pleased to let you know, that we won and the issue is dead. Great job Cameron. I look forward to seeing you back at Corporate."

Cameron was not completely surprised when the law department outbid every other division for his service, but he was very pleased by how much they set his starting salary, yearly bonus, and stock options.

Sitting in his mid-size corporate office in 1980, Cameron was the first and only black employee. Affirmative action had no bearing on Cameron's hire. Race was obviously an issue, otherwise there would have been more blacks and people of color long before Cameron. Some people could easily fail in a hostile employment environment, but not Cameron. The creed of the Tuskegee Airmen of being the best, pushed Cameron to succeed. Cameron believed success in the corporate world would motivate him to be the best.

"Cameron, you have a natural talent for working on legislation. I have a position that I think would be perfect for you," said the General Counsel. "Would you be interested in being our company lobbyist in Washington State?"

"Absolutely Sir, when do I start?" Cameron laughed to himself as he had zero idea what a corporate lobbyist did.

"Great. I will send a few letters to other big corporations, letting them know that I have assigned you to work with them in Olympia. Good luck Cameron. Keep me posted on your progress."

The very next day, the Director of Employment Relations walked into Cameron's office and said, "I hear you have been asked to be our lobbyist in Washington State. Are there any issues that you may not support?"

"Yes Sir, I will not support anything illegal and I will not block or oppose racial progress,"

"Anything else?" inquired the Director.

Cameron knew that the corporate senior executives wanted to know if they could count on the first black man in their corporate facilities to be a team player. "Yes. I pledge to give 200% effort to support the mission of the corporation," said Cameron.

"Thank you," said the Director as he left Cameron's office.

Cameron sat in his chair wondering if he had just thrown a wrench in his lobbyist position.

He learned the answer two weeks later when he met with the most powerful business lobbyists in Washington State. They all met at an exclusive mens golf club near Wenatchee, Washington. It was 1980 and no women or minorities could be members or play golf. The lobbyists were shocked beyond belief when Cameron entered the room wearing his three-piece suit. They wore golf attire. Clothing wasn't what shocked the men, it was the fact the Cameron was black. Men that entered the room after Cameron sat as far away as possible from Cameron. After the morning business meeting, the lobbyists adjourned to eat lunch and then play golf. Given this was the first meeting with the lobbyists, not one person invited Cameron to join them for lunch or to play golf, even if it was at a different golf course. It should be noted that Cameron had learned that the lobbyists liked to play golf following their business meetings. He had borrowed his mother's old golf clubs. Cameron as a teenager used the clubs to play a round or two. He was not a great golfer. He was not even good. He did have his mother's 1950 set of golf clubs in the trunk of his car had anyone invited him to play.

Cameron was so furious at the hatred shown to him that he got into his car and headed back to Seattle. As he drove along the highway, he thought how he would tell the General Counsel that he was quitting his new position as a lobbyist. Cameron drove approximately 20 miles when his thoughts turned to his father. Did his father ever quit? No! This was horrible, however this was nothing compared to how horrible it was for his father and all the other Tuskegee Airmen in World War II. So, Cameron turned the car around and participated in the meetings the next day where no one said a word to Cameron.

Turning the clock forward five years, Cameron became the president of this business lobbyist organization, where he determined where the meetings would be held (no discrimination clubs) and where he would have the final word on how much money all candidates for state office would receive. Of special note, Cameron was elected and re-elected as president for ten years in a row. No one before or since served a longer term than Cameron. These years in the business legislative history would come to be known as the golden business years. Business thrived in the low tax environment. Job growth exploded and salaries increased. Cameron effectively focused the election of pro-business candidates.

By now the Price household had expanded to three beautiful children: Sage, Anthony, and Mark. Michelle loved being a mom and loved her children. Holding each child, Cameron knew this was what God had in store for him. His children were so precious. They looked absolutely adorable. He took turns dancing with them. Music had definitely changed from the Motown love songs, but the 1960s music still captured Cameron's musical heart. The kids loved to be held by their father as he danced with them. It was now 1985. It would be very difficult to select the number one song for the 80s, but here is round up of Cameron's top three songs:

1. USA for Africa, *We are the World*, Michael Jackson
2. Michael Jackson, *Billy Jean*, Epic record Label
3. Whitney Houston, *Saving All My Love for You*, Arista record Label

Cameron, lying on his back, held one of his kids from his shoulder above his head and would take turns flying the kids in the air to his favorite music saying Superman or Superwoman. The kids screamed with such pleasure.

He taught Sage, his daughter, when she was 14-month-old, a game to impress his relatives and friends. "Sage," he asked.

"Yes, DaDa"

"I understand you know calculus?"

"Yes, DaDa, I know calculus."

"No way, you are too young to know calculus."

"Yes, DaDa, I know calculus."

"Okay, spell calculus for me."

"C,A,L,C,U,L,U,S," said Sage.

"Well, maybe you can spell calculus, but you don't know how it works."

"I do DaDa."

"Ok Sage, what is the square root of 9?"

"That is easy DaDa, everyone one knows it is 3."

"Ok Sage, what is the derivative of 9?"

"That is easy too DaDa, it is 0!"

Sage not only impressed friends and family but she went on to impress her high school math teachers where she graduated near the top of her class and she was seated number one in her freshman math class in College.

Cameron and Michelle purchased a large $210,000 4-bedroom home in an all-white upper-class neighborhood. Sage and their two sons, Anthony, and Mark loved, the big back yard swing, hot tub, and sauna that Cameron had built. Sage was so cute and the boys were so handsome. They played in the hot tub where Cameron told them amazing stories about a captain on a space ship named "No-butts" in a galaxy far into the future, who battled aliens to keep the last piece of American freedom alive.

"Daddy, tell us another story," they asked while splashing hot water.

Their neighbors were really friendly and one neighbor walked up to Cameron, who had just gotten out of his car in the drive-way, and said "I saw the darndest thing at your house a few minutes ago." "I always thought when you move into a house, items move into the house. Well, when I saw items being moved out of your house, I went to investigate. I saw three men jump into a large green truck when the saw me and they took off quickly." Cameron and Michelle had been burglarized. Cameron wished that he could have been there when the burglars had entered their house. From law school, he learned that you cannot put a loaded spiked spring gun to impale burglars' hell bent on breaking in and stealing your things, but a crouching 4th degree black belt would be a different story.

Cameron didn't lose that much thanks to his watchful neighbor.

Fortunately, they were able to replace all the stolen items with the exception of the irreplaceable beautiful stereo system that he had purchased in the Philippines.

Cameron had a special note to minorities: in many ways, the stock market is like a math class. If you do your research on a company trending sales forecasts and management skills, your investments like the answer to a math question does not discriminate. "Invest and make big returns is the key to getting out of the discrimination maze thereby allowing you to do what you want to achieve." It is the key to self-actualization. Michelle countered and said to many people, "Cam, money is not important. It is religion and the belief in a higher power that are important." "Absolutely," said Cameron, "but you need food and shelter which can be a challenge in many communities."

"Cam, Big El is on the phone."

Big El and Susan, called Cameron and Michelle with the exciting news that they had a boy named Jack. They said he was a big handsome baby with a great big smile with blonde hair and blue eyes.

"I couldn't think of a better name than Jack," said Cameron. "Let's get together soon buddy."

Cameron's life as a Fortune 500 Corporate lobbyist was great. He practically had an unlimited expense account eating at expensive restaurants and drinking the finest of beverages. He had access to the company's Lear Jets. He took Michelle and his three kids whenever possible with him. They stayed in luxurious hotels and resorts.

By now, all the lobbyists and legislators knew that Cameron was a poor golfer and an easy mark to make money. Cameron became known as the oilman. Every shot he took, he dug enough dirt out of the ground where everyone expected a gusher of oil to come shooting out of the ground. They made lots of money off him until another organization that he chaired, embarrassed to see Cameron's old 1950s golf clubs, bought him a full set of deluxe golf clubs and a golf bag. Slowly Cameron's golf game changed to where he started to break even on his wagers.

One of the most powerful lobbyists in Washington State had special words for Cameron when they were alone. "Yes boy," I think this is the best approach, or "no boy," we don't want to that."

What an insult this was to Cameron. He knew he should tell him to cease, or knock it off, but he never said a thing. Cameron always looked him in the face and politely smiled at this most overtly racist man in his lobbying circle. Instead of pushing Cameron to fail, it motivated him to succeed by being one of the best lobbyists. Where some might falter, this was reminiscent of the grocery store owner near Tuskegee trying to whip Cameron's father, Dan, during flight school. Dan never backed away and now Cameron never backed away.

Cameron also learned, if you want to be better than a good lobbyist, you must save your corporation a ton of money. Cameron thrived in Olympia, quietly winning legislative issues favorable to his company.

The General Counsel of his corporation proudly shared Cameron's legislative achievement in Washington State with the Board of Directors and the CEO. Subsequently, Cameron was promoted and given total lobbyist responsibility for all fifty states.

The good news was that Cameron received a salary increase but the bad news was that he had not received any additional staff and he began to lose influence with the power lobbyists in Olympia who could no longer count on Cameron's help on pressing legislative battles. Cameron might be in Montana or West Virginia when battles were being fought in Olympia. He learned to quickly figure out solutions by contacting key legislators and lobbyists resulting in favorable legislation being enacted. These days reminded him of the rapid-fire pace in the Philippines where he tracked the advancing movement of enemy targets. Life as a fifty-state lobbyist now was very challenging for Cameron as he did his very best to make ever minute count.

Cameron was turning into a power lobbyist. Interestingly, being a corporate lobbyist for a big corporation was an outstanding career move for Cameron. Most people do not know what they want to do when they grow up. Becoming a lobbyist was like a duck finding water. He loved politics and he loved changing or modifying laws that other attorneys had to follow. Cameron had found the perfect job.

# Chapter 11

# Cameron's Six Degrees of Separation

**"H**i son," said Cameron's father. "I would like you and your family to join us on a family reunion with our Canadian relatives. Children of Debra, your great grandmother Aretha's cousin, moved from Washington State to Canada years ago in search of better jobs and to escape bigotry and racism. They are going to have a family reunion at the Fairmont Hotel in Vancouver, B.C."

"Sounds fun dad. I will talk with Michelle and get back to you."

Michelle thought it would be a fantastic opportunity to meet a side of Cameron's family that they had never met and their young kids might have the opportunity to take in the world-famous Vancouver Zoo.

The next month, they followed Cameron's father and stepmother in their car through the Canadian Border station and into Vancouver. The hotel was nice and there were wonderful areas for the kids to play and explore.

All the relatives were so kind and hugged Michelle, Sage, Anthony, Mark, and Cameron.

The banquet room was filled with delicious appetizers, main courses of steak and rack of lamb, lobsters, and sweet desserts.

All the relatives knew that Cameron's father was a jet pilot in World War II, having served with the famous Tuskegee Airmen. Everyone was so proud of Cameron's Father. Dan was a decorated

Tuskegee pilot who took no crap from anyone. When you put your life on the line day in and day out to fight Italian and German pilots in the name of freedom, listening to racist comments anywhere was not tolerated. Dan had told many disparaging souls to burn in hell. Cameron was so proud of his father.

The Canadian relatives were also very proud of Cameron as he was the first in the clan to graduate from law school and become a corporate lawyer.

Cameron and Michelle were so happy to meet their relatives. One special young lady who was so beautiful was their step-cousin Monica. She told them of their journey to Canada and the activities of many of her relatives.

Cameron learned of Debra's difficult path to freedom in Canada. Canadians were much more tolerant of blacks; however, jobs were not plentiful and high paying jobs without an education did not exist. Heavy fork lifters, yard workers, and shoeshine men were jobs that were more readily available. If one had the talent, entry into the entertainment field was possible.

Another relative asked Cameron, "while I'm certain many of our laws are different, would it be okay if I called you about questions I have on starting a business?"

"Please do," responded Cameron.

Cameron was so happy to meet his Canadian relatives who looked so much like him. What he learned next nearly floored him.

In life, there is a prophetic statement that says we are all related to each other by six degrees of separation.

Cameron had just learned that he was a distant relative, make that a step-cousin, of one of the most famous guitar musicians of all time, Big Quincy Noble who had died in 1970. What a journey it had been for two single black women in 1908 from Marshall, Texas to travel to Seattle where one would have a grandson that would help win World War II as a Tuskegee Airmen and the other moved to Canada and had a step-grandson who would be recognized as one of the greatest left handed guitarists in the world. Debra's daughter moved to Vancouver and would eventually marry a gentleman who had two sons, Big Quincy Noble and Sebastion Rock.

Michelle and Cameron also learned that their step-cousin, Sebastian Rock, was the lead singer in a famous Canadian Band which was playing later that evening in Gas Town. They were given tickets and Cameron's father and stepmother said they would watch the kids.

The rock concert took place in a huge auditorium that was completely sold out as fans eagerly paid high prices for scalped tickets. When the music started to play, it was raw and upbeat. The kaleidoscope of colors flashing around the room were beautiful. The fans cheered! Everyone was ready for a big party tonight.

Cameron's step-cousin sang his heart out and the audience showed their appreciation by clapping and dancing to his music.

During the final set, Sebatian held a mike, said "Ladies and Gentlemen, I am so proud to have many of my relatives from America here tonight." "Family, please come up on stage and join me."

Michelle, Cameron, and several other relatives walked up to the stage with the crowd cheering.

Sebastion began to sing his number one signature song, *Love*, and the crowd went wild. He danced and the music played on.

Michelle was a very good dancer, and Cameron danced to the funky beat of the music and then something happened. Cameron had been away from karate for five plus years, but he had not forgotten his karate dance moves. It was a special slow-motion movement where Cameron's lightning fast kicks and dance steps combined with Sebastion's throbbing beat of beautiful music sent the crowd in a raging roar of appreciation.

Later Cameron's cousin asked, "where did you learn to dance like that?"

Cameron said, "I am a 4th degree black belt with an attitude."

"I want you in my shows," he said with a smile.

On the drive back to Seattle, Cameron thought about his wonderful Canadian relatives that he met and his famous distant cousin, Big Quincy Noble. What if he had lived longer, he thought? What would his next great song be like. Cameron actually started to put his code breaking skill to the task, when he came to the conclusion that his guitar playing step-cousin, Big Quincy Noble, had played his best music, he had died, and he shouldn't try to alter anything.

# Chapter 12

# A Tuskegee Airman's Adventure following World War II

The Tuskegee Airmen in World War II were not just good or damn good pilots, they were they best! The experiment to see if these black pilots could fly resulted in major victories in Africa, Italy, and Germany. White bomber pilots began requesting these black pilots to protect them on their bombing flights. Historical documents indicate the Tuskegee pilots never lost a bomber. Maybe one or two, but from staggering bomber losses to nearly none, these Tuskegee pilots deserve a gold star in history for helping end World War II. Eventually, their heroic efforts resulted in President Truman signing Executive order 9981 on July 26, 1948, directing equality of treatment and opportunity in all of the United States Armed Forces. This was a significant step toward racial integration throughout the United States of America. On March 29, 2007, President George W. Bush and Congress awarded the Congressional Gold Medal to the Tuskegee Airmen. Speaking on behalf of the Tuskegee Airmen, Dr. Roscoe Brown, a former commander of the 100th Fighter Squadron, 332nd Fighter Group, thanked Bush and the House and Senate for "voting to award this medal collectively to the pilots, bombardiers, the navigators, the mechanics, the ground officers, the enlisted men and women who served with the Tuskegee Airmen."

As the years passed following World War II, Cameron's father Dan kept in close contact with his Tuskegee friends. Approximately 14 Tuskegee airmen lived in Washington State and they frequently stopped by to visit him. Many more airmen from nearby states also dropped by for regional Tuskegee reunions. Cameron listened as the men shared their great flying adventures. He also heard how difficult it was for these men to provide for their families following their military careers.

Dan owned several planes following his service in the Air Force. He owned several Piper and Cessna single engine planes as well as two amphibian planes. His favorite was his Piper 400 Camache with 4 seats, low wings, all metal, light aircraft, retractable landing gear, and could carry 130 US Gallons of fuel before providing for additional fuel storage containers. The base price for a 1964 Piper 400 Camache was $28,750. He loved flying and enjoyed his many fishing and hunting adventures throughout the state of Washington and Canada.

After years of hearing of white men and white women flying perilous journeys around the world, Dan decided that he would embark on a flight around the world.

"Son," said Dan, "our country needs black heroes. I think I am up to the challenge of flying a single engine plane around the world. It may be very difficult but I know if anyone can do it, I can do it. I am going to call it, 'an air excursion around the world in a single engine plane by a Tuskegee Airmen'."

Cameron wanted to join his dad's adventure but his young family and work schedule were too much responsibility to break away for that amount of time.

Dan meticulously chartered a course from Seattle to Greenland, Europe, Africa, Asia, and on to Seattle. To raise publicity for this event, he wrote a letter to the Scientific Journal to see if they would commission him for the pictures he would take along his journey as well as the story he would write. Dan thought it might take several months to hear back from the magazine. What shocked him was he heard back in less than a week. He received a short one sentence letter that said, "No," and not even a "no thanks."

Dan had the funds, so he decided to go on his adventure without any endorsements.

David, Dan's youngest brother, jumped at his brother's invitation to join him on the historic aviation journey. David asked if he could take his oldest son, Brent. David thought this trip of a life time might motivate and inspire his son to achieve his greatest dreams. David firmly believed that even one great life experience could shape a person's life. If they successfully flew a plane around the world, the experience could make a huge positive difference in their lives and it might stimulate others to make a real difference in society.

Dan agreed and Brent joined them.

Later, David shared the following comments about his brother's epic flight. "We both know how your father always meticulously planned for hunting and fishing trips reviewing weather reports, lake and mountain climates, and flight plans. But I had never before seen your father so engaged in the technical details of a flight. Attention to detail was of paramount importance. Weight of food and supplies were measured to the ounce. Additionally, he ensured that he had more than enough fuel to fly from one landing field to the next. He even adopted safety measures in case they encountered equipment failure along the path. Dan wrote down every step and committed them to memory. Custom Border stations, where they would seek entry, were clearly marked on the map to save time.

On a warm June morning in 1988, their wheels lifted up and Dan, David, and Brent took off from Boeing Airfield in Seattle. They were in contact with air traffic controllers on every leg of their trip. They flew approximately 15,000 to 20,000 feet high. They passed over huge mountain ranges, lakes, waterfalls, and rivers seeing beautiful fauna and birds. Dan, David, and Brent looked down at the most amazing and beautiful terrain that was a blanket of yellow, green, and brown.

They stopped along the way to refuel. It was a magical flight as they reached their designated targets. Greenland and Great Britain landings were within minutes of Dan's targeted landing times. The trip was challenging for everyone on the plane especially the sore backs and leg muscles from sitting in a stationary position for so long.

Abruptly, everything changed when the engine started to sputter. They had sufficient fuel so something mechanical was going on.

They were over the Middle East. Dan told David they had to be somewhere over Iran. As the engine continue to sputter, Dan noticed an Iranian jet pulling up beside him. The jet was approximately 30 feet off their left-wing and it's pilot began pointing down with his hand. Iran at the time had strained relationships with the United States. Dan aggressively looked at the map and figured if they could travel approximately 10 more miles, they would be in Pakistan, a safer country.

Dan gently lowered the plane's altitude giving the appearance that he was landing. The Iranian jet pilot would have nothing to do with it. The pilot proceeded to fall behind Dan's plane and shot bullets towards them. Fortunately, no one was killed or hurt. Even though the plane continued to sputter, Dan knew that they were trapped, so he rapidly took the plane down and landed on an airfield in the desert.

Two Jeeps full of Iranian soldiers with camouflage uniforms and rifles ordered Dan and the men into their vehicles. Several minutes later, they were dragged inside a cement block building, where the soldiers began to interrogate them. In their heavy Iranian accents, they ask, "You are Americans, yes?"

"Yes," said Dan.

"You are CIA?"

"No. We are tourists," Dan replied.

"Don't give us that crap."

"Black men do not have airplanes, you are CIA!"

They were kicked and beaten badly. Over and over again they were asked, "What is your mission? What do you want? Who do you work for?"

Brent, David's son, who was along for the adventure of a life time, never thought in a million years, that this might happen to him. "If I get out of this alive God, I promise I will be a good young man. I promise."

The beatings continued into the next day. It must've been well over 115° in that cement block building in the desert.

One of the soldiers asked Dan how he had learned to fly since he had never seen a black man fly.

Feeling the painful bruises all over his body, Dan said that he had been a pilot in World War II, and flew his jet here in the middle east against the Germans to free the people of Iran.

"Yes. I heard something of this. If we release you, where do you intend to go?"

Dan said, "India."

The soldier, who appeared to be in charge said, "No! We will release you by sending you to Tehran where you will fly back to America. We will seize your plane. It is now our plane."

The men were taken into a small room and fed soup and a small piece of bread. Later that evening they were herded into a vehicle and driven through the desert to Tehran. They were released into the custody of an Iranian airport military official.

Dan told his brother that he had no intentions of turning over his expensive plane to the Iranians. "Do you want to go back and get my plane with me?"

David said, "No! I have my son with us. David continued by saying I think I will take him back to the United States and call this trip an adventure of a lifetime. I will take the safe journey from here. I never dreamed we would be shot at and beaten."

When the commercial plane designated by the Iranian officials was ready for departure for Turkey, Dan told the official he was sick and could not fly. He said he would take the next plane and said his goodbyes to his brother and nephew.

After the plane safely departed, Dan went into the men's restroom and climbed out the window. He walked rapidly down the road where he reached a market bazaar. He gave a merchant several US dollars for a white Muslim robe and hat. Looking like a black Lawrence of Arabia in his white garb, Dan searched repair shops near the airport for an air filter to replace the troubled part on his plane. Fortunately, he found such a part at one of the repair shops. With his new clothes, Dan blended in with the Iranian crowd. He hired a man with a car to take him to the airfield in the desert. As they drove out of town, Dan noticed vehicles with flashing blue lights obviously looking for him.

It was a long dusty journey back to the airfield. Eventually he saw the airfield about 3 miles down the road and he told the driver to stop. Dan paid him more than he asked and thanked him with a wave of his hand.

Dan walked off the desert road and hid behind mounds of desert sand until dark. The hot desert temperature was now rapidly cooling. He did not see any wildlife including the ever-present scorpions in the inhospitable desert.

As darkness engulfed the land, Dan walked towards the airfield. He did not see a sentry, but he did see that his plane was still there. He slowly walked to his plane and carefully touched the wings and tail to ascertain whether or not it would be safe to fly. While there were two bullet holes, he did not believe that they would prevent the plane from flying. The landing gear was not tied down. He opened up the engine compartment and carefully replaced the air filter. Running his finger over the old filter he knew he had made a correct assessment about the sand clogging the air filter.

In the dead of night, Dan climbed into his plane, turned on the engine and raced down the airfield. The lights over the compound turned on as Dan's plane lifted off the ground. He turned the lights on the plane only after he figured he was over Pakistan.

On the ground in Pakistan, he assessed whether or not his plane could continue on the voyage around the world. The bullet holes were too destructive to the integrity of the plane so he canceled the journey. It took some time, but he found a ship that could haul his plane back to the United States.

The around the world flight would have to take place on another day. Dan, David, Brent, and the airplane all made it safely back to the United States.

Dan would later make one more attempt at being the first black man to fly around the world in a single engine aircraft.

# Chapter 13

# Big El is Injured during an Arrest

"Hey Cam, you are not going to believe what happened to me," said Big El.

"Wait. I don't think I will like what you're about to tell me. It's sounds similarly to how you told me you were involved in a car crash in Greece."

"I was involved in a car crash and more," said Big El.

"Here's what happened to me yesterday. I received a call that a bank robbery had taken place not far from me. I sat in my car and jotted down a brief description of the car and the suspect. Moments later, the car and suspect passed me. I turned on my overhead lights and siren, and gave chase.

"It was a cold winter morning with snow and ice all over the ground. When he noticed me, he rapidly increased his speed flying down the icy roads. I almost disengaged the chase as there were several cars and pedestrians along the way. But I saw a stretch of road where there were no cars and pedestrians and I pushed my squad car into overdrive until I rear-ended the suspect's vehicle. He spun out of control doing donuts until he slid to a stop.

"He jumped out of his car and ran up a hill hoping to get to a heavily forested area for his escape. I saw he had a gun in his hand and I could've shot him, but instead, I fired two shots near his head. He stopped and threw his gun on the ground.

"I told him to kick the gun away from him, which he did.

"I then ordered him to get down on the ground and lie on his stomach. As I reached for his wrist to put the cuffs on, he jumped up and a fight ensued.

"He was a bulky guy about six feet and about 230 pounds. He knocked me backwards on the ice and I jumped to reach his gun, but I slid. Man, I landed hard on the ice. It felt like I broke something.

"He stretched to reach his gun. In spite of the pain, Cam you never saw me move so fast. I grabbed his pant leg and dragged him back before he could grab his gun that was just inches away from his hand.

"I took out my revolver and pointed it at him and said, 'the next move you make is either going to take you to the undertaker or to jail. What's it going to be?'

"With his nose, flat on the ground I put the cuffs on him. We walked back to the squad car and I put him in the backseat. I radioed ahead for backup letting the dispatcher know I caught the suspect and was in a little pain from hitting the ice on the ground.

"When my backup arrived, I informed him I had hurt my back chasing the suspect. He took the suspect and put him in his car and called in to get a medic vehicle over for me.

"As I laid back in my front seat the pain started surging through my back. I grimaced and then noticed that my car was blocking the road, so I turned on the engine to turn my car around to park it along side of the road.

"As I turned the engine on, my beast of a machine went into overdrive and started speeding down the road. Finally, it stopped. Susan had said for years that we needed new cars.

"The day had finally come that my life was seriously in danger by this broken down death trap on wheels. I managed to turn off the engine with the key. Suddenly, I noticed a car approaching me at a high rate of speed. The driver obviously noticed me and slammed on the brakes but the momentum on the ice caused it to continue straight towards me. I tried to turn my engine on and move my car but the car would not start and the car slammed into me hard. Cam I think my bruised bones became broken bones in my spine."

"How you doing now?"

"Well, right now I'm doing pretty good. The doctor has me on morphine and some other medicine so I'm not feeling too bad."

Big El would go on to have six back surgeries with ever-increasing dependency on alcohol and painkillers. When he wasn't at the hospital or at home he worked at a desk job which he hated.

Susan and their wonderful son Jack each supported Big El through the painful times with their love.

# Chapter 14

# Cameron, the Truth Shall Set You Free

C ameron sat behind the wheel of his 1985 Audi Quattro on his way to purchase a rare, vintage, expensive fly rod in the Capitol Hill neighborhood of Seattle. The rod sounded perfect for the price. Cameron and his corporate friend, Drew, were about to go fishing in a lake in western Canada where the trout were big, fat, and hungry. Drew also had a vintage fly rod, so Cameron could not believe his good fortune when he saw a similar rod advertised in the newspaper.

On the drive from Tacoma, Cameron thought about his loving and beautiful wife and his cherished children. Cam was so happy that he had waited for that special someone. The children were getting bigger. Life was happy.

He wondered if he would always have to strive harder, going the extra mile, in order to crack the all-white glass ceiling to become a successful senior executive businessman in America.

He also thought about how he might stay connected with his injured best friend, Big El, who lived so far away on the East Coast.

Lastly, Cameron was fascinated with a new study to discover one's ancestors through DNA testing. Cameron guessed that he was black, white, and native American. He wanted to know the makeup of his ancestry. The study seemed a little expensive, but if Michelle concurred with him, he thought he might sign up for the analysis later that week.

As he neared Seattle, a new and favorite song of Cameron's started playing on the radio. It was *Bolero* by Maurice Ravel. The seventeen minutes of dramatic, ever increasing, syncopation resonated within Cameron. As the music played Cameron felt that Bolero had a tragic side, almost like a warning to him, with the loud melodic snare drum as if soldiers were marching in a battle field preparing to face their ultimate destiny. Love and death, the opening and closing of one's heart and one's mind.

Cameron got off the freeway and proceeded up Denny Street turning left on Broadway then right on East Thomas street. Capitol Hill, was a densely residential district in Seattle filled with stately homes. His mother had taken him to Volunteer Park and the Asian Art museum when he was a young boy. He gave some thought about where he might eat after he purchased the fly rod. He narrowed the selection between an old favorite called Dicks, the home of the original nineteen cent hamburger, also known for their great fries and shakes or he might go to the famous La Brindisi Restaurant for a special feast of New Orleans' food like red beans, rice and Jambalaya.

He now figured that he was about three blocks from his destination. As he passed 12th Street, something told him to look down the alley that he was passing on the left. He saw a police car about three hundred yards down the long alley. Cameron looked at the car and knew what was about to happen. He drove to the nearest parking strip along the curb and immediately pulled over. He got out of his car and sat on the front hood of his car as the policeman drove up to him and turned on his siren,

"Get back in your car," he screamed.

Cameron asked, "What have I done?"

"Get back in your car." The policeman took out his gun and pointed it at Cameron. "I won't tell you again, get back in your car."

Cameron heard the police officer's command and walked back and sat in his car. Seeing the gun pointed directly at him, Cameron's mind raced with thoughts of the how this situation would play out and what he should do. First of all the cop had no apparent reason to pull him over. Cameron still wanted to know what he had done. Cameron gave measured thought to a scenario if the officer got close enough with the gun still pointing at him what were the possibilities of a fourth-degree black belt taking the gun from him.

What if he killed the police officer in the struggle for the gun. Cameron's mind raced faster. Even if he disarmed the cop and rendered him incapacitated, he would probably spend years in jail. Police officers have badges and uniforms and have a sworn duty to protect citizens so juries nearly always support police officers in lawsuits brought by citizens and in criminal trial brought by prosecutors.

This cop was unscrupulous in pretending that Cameron had done something illegal when he had not. Maybe cops should be held to a standard of three strikes and it is life in prison for lying, planting a gun or knife, saying that a defendant committed a violation when he or she had not, stealing drugs from drug traffickers, and taking drug money.

But isn't one negative strike by a police officer too many? How many negative strikes should a cop be allowed to gather. Cameron definitely thought of Big El, so he knew that all cops were not dishonest and probably most cops were very honest.

Cameron's mind was now in full throttle. Cameron's father had never talked to him about what to do if he were pulled over by a cop. He wished he had. Cameron knew that society would spin out of control without the courage and bravery of the men and women of law enforcement.

In an instant, Cameron had now come full circle in determining how to deal with a dishonest cop.

Cameron's code to break free from a dishonest cop is as follows:

First, know the names of the police chief, mayor, and governor. Tell the cop you are close personal friends of all three public servants. Maybe, not surprisingly, this may make the cop mad when you tell him as he could dislike the thought of you having more power than the officer. This may not help in preventing the infraction from being charged, but it will help to remove the cop's finger on the trigger.

Second, each state has a fallen officer dinner fund to raise money for fallen officers and their families. So, before you ever get into a car, be sure to send a contribution to this fund. Then, when you get pulled over by a policeman, mention that you help by raising funds for fallen officers and their families. Again, the purpose is to dial back the finger on the trigger.

The cop did holster his gun and said that he saw Cameron drive straight at a corner which was a right hand turn only.

"You couldn't see me from where you were parked in the alley," Cameron said loudly.

"Oh, I see you are a trouble maker," said the cop. "I am going to call for back-up," screamed the cop.

Back-up arrived shortly and now two officers approached Cameron's driver side window.

"Give me your driver's license, proof of insurance, and your social security number."

"Excuse me officer," as Cameron talked to the backup officer, "Am I required to give my social security number on a routine traffic offense?"

"Yes," said the officer.

Cameron had never heard of this requirement but gave the information to the police.

The officers literally spent thirty minutes digging and digging to find some offense so they could arrest him. They found nothing.

The bad cop presented Cameron with a ticket for failure to turn right at the corner and told Cameron to sign the ticket.

Cameron signed the ticket, but added the words, signed under protest.

The bad cop said loudly, that is not his signature, let's take him down to jail.

The backup cop said, "That's his signature, let's go."

Both officers departed in their vehicles.

With his ticket in hand, Cameron drove to the site where the officer claimed he should have made a right hand turn.

He noticed a sign that read: Due to construction activity, all vehicles may turn left, right or they may drive straight ahead.

Cameron drove straight ahead and noticed the dishonest cop again, no doubt writing his notes on the ticket that he had given Cameron. With the passenger side window rolled down, he approached the policeman whose window was also rolled down and said, "You are a very dishonest cop, and I think I caught you."

Michelle heard what Cameron had said to the cop and said she was surprised that the cop hadn't shot him.

Later, Cameron called the city highway and construction department to find out if the construction turn sign on the corner was valid. The sign was valid and had been placed in its space four days before Cameron received his ticket. The department engineer said he would send a letter with the pertinent information. Cameron also called the city's police department internal affairs office to report the police officer misconduct. Cameron, called and left messages with the police chief, mayor, and governor. He went back to where he was pulled over and put signs asking if anyone had heard the cop yelling at Cameron. No one called him. He did receive a call from the police department's internal affairs later, who said they found nothing and considered the case closed.

"Interesting" said Cameron, to the Internal Affairs' officer, "You are closing the case and I have a bombshell of a letter indicating that your cop was lying."

"Oh, please Mr. Price, send us a copy of that letter," asked the internal affairs officer.

Sensing corruption by internal affairs to protect all of the officers of the police department, Cameron said, "No, Let's let the judge look at it and make the decision,

Several weeks passed and Cameron stood before the judge as his case was about to be heard. "Your honor," said the bailiff, "Neither the charging officer nor anyone from the police department are here. We just have a note indicating the police department does not wish to pursue the infraction."

The judge said, "You won Mr. Price."

"Excuse me, your honor, this is not a win. I want to have a full hearing where I can bring to light the misdeeds and activities of our police department," said Cameron.

"You don't understand, Mr. Price, you won and there is nothing more for you to do."

Cameron was upset about these chains of events until he received a letter from the mayor's office indicating the mayor had reviewed the case. He indicated that he had looked at the construction activity report. He also found two neighbors who heard the cop screaming at Cameron, and he saw where the cop had lied on the ticket.

"Mr. Price, we do not want this type of individual serving in our community and as such, I have fired the police officer effective three days ago!!

So, the moral of this relevant story is to live to talk another day. You may be wrongly accused of a crime, but don't let the feeling of being a caged rabbit kill you. It doesn't matter what color you are.

Keep searching for the truth, which will set you free.

Lastly, the 'Ten Golden Keys' to success:

1. Study Karate.
2. Work hard: You can achieve anything you desire, if you are willing to work exceedingly hard and smart for it.
3. Go to college.
4. Dress for success at interviews, looking exactly like the person doing the interviewing.
5. One's aspiration is predicated by using your mental and physical abilities.
6. Never get divorced.
7. Pick your friends by the action of their minds and their hearts.
8. Be a great leader by being smart, honest, having a strong charismatic character, loyal to the team, and developing the team to win.
9. Know true love: For a man, it is when time stands still, an irresistible magnetic force moves you to that special someone, and both your heart and mind start dancing in your body, anything short of this is a play date. A woman should take careful time to analyze her wants and desires in a man. True love has to not only fill each and every one of her desires, but her desires must be filled each and every day and night. A woman needs a man who can adapt to her changes.
10. Be Spiritual.

The Black Skeleton Key No. 1:
**Never do drugs!**

# Character List in Alphabetical Order

- Abrianna — Beautiful high-fashion New York model who Cameron met in Italy
- Amy — Beautiful Canadian lady who Cameron met in Italy
- Anthony — Cameron's son
- Arthur — Cameron's service friend made famous in Mexico
- Aunt Olive — Cameron's aunt on his mother's side
- Aunt Vine — Cameron's aunt on his mother's side
- Baroni — Big El's State Patrol friend
- Bauden — Football player in the Philippines
- Benjamin — Cameron's step-brother
- Betty — Susan's mother
- Big El (Elston Royal) — Cameron's best friend
- Bill — Cameron's corporate friend
- Blaze — Cameron's corporate friend
- Brad — Cameron's cousin
- Brent — Cameron's cousin
- Camel — Big El's and Cameron's victory high five sign

- Cameron — Main Character. Book based on his life.
- Carol — Cameron's father's sister (aunt)
- Chaplin — Fellow student and Cameron's drinking friend
- Christian Sharpen — Big El's groomsman
- Dan — Cameron's father
- Darlene Thomas — Calculus tutor
- David — Cameron's youngest uncle on his father's side
- Debra — Cameron's Great-grandmother
- Doug — Service friend, who he met in basic training in San Antonio Texas. He wanted to play the saxophone in the Air Force band
- Dr Avner — Gave Big El his first job after the Air Force
- Drew — Cameron's corporate friend
- Flint — Cameron's step-father
- Gerald — Washington State Bar Exam Study Partner
- Granny — Susan's grandmother
- GW — Service buddy who loved golf and women
- Happy — Black waiter who served Big El his favorite food
- Irene — Nelson's wife
- Judge Boudin — Tacoma Superior Court Judge
- Katie Capriana — Cameron's friend from high school
- Kora — Cameron's past girlfriend
- Kurt — Friend in stock marketing class and Law school

- Larry Junior — Susan's brother
- Larry Senior — Susan's father
- Laura — Nelson's girlfriend
- Louisa — Daughter of a friend of great aunt Mary
- Marina — Cameron's Italian landlord Michael's wife
- Mark — Cameron's son
- Mary — Cameron's great aunt on mother's side
- Mary Dane — Big El's younger sister
- Maxwell — Service friend accidentally stabbed by Cameron
- Michael — Cameron's landlord in Italy
- Michelle — Cameron's wife
- Minister Robinson — Michelle's family minister
- Mississippi — Service friend (basic training through the Philippines)
- Monica — Cameron's step-cousin
- Morgan — Sharon and Cameron's son
- Nelson — Cameron's childhood friend
- Paul — Cameron's corporate friend
- Peter — Big El's neighbor
- Polly — Stair climbing friend at North University
- Priscilla — Cameron's grandmother
- Quincy Noble — Cameron'a step-cousin
- Ray — Law school friend
- Robin — Friend from Italy
- Sage — Cameron's daughter
- Sally — Cameron's corporate friend
- Sensei Marshall — Cameron's karate instructor

- Sebastion Rock — Cameron's step-cousin
- Sharon — Cameron's girlfriend before joining the Air Force
- Susan — Big El's girlfriend then wife
- Susie — Arthur's wife
- Ted — Big El's cousin-in-law
- Terrence — Cameron's great uncle on mother's side
- Trista — Big El's Canadian friend who he met in Italy
- Uncle General — Cameron's uncle on his mother's side
- Uncle Lionist — Cameron's uncle on his mother's side
- Uncle Lloyd — Preacher who married Michelle and Cameron
- Uncle Paige Jr — Cameron's uncle on his mother's side.
- Uncle Thas — Cameron's uncle on his mother's side
- Uncle Wyman — Cameron's uncle on his mother's side
- Walter — Aunt Carol's husband
- Warren — Cameron's uncle on his father's side